# When I Was Green

T.S. Dawson

## Acknowledgements

Thank you to all who have supported my writing these last two years. Were it not for your encouragement and, the fact that you give your time to my writing, there'd be no need to put all of those who've helped me to the trouble of these endeavors.

Thank you to Donna Goss for continuing to push me on and to lend an ear whenever I need to talk trough the occasional writer's block. Thank you for continuing to be my first editor. Also, thank you for holding my hand through The Decatur Book Festival and the arts shows this last year.

Thank you to Scott Meeks for taking on the project of cleaning up my vocabulary and making everything better. Thank you for giving your time to help us edit. Also, thank you for helping with our social media campaign and filling in where needed.

Thank you to Christie Johnson for continuing to help us with editing and for helping to get the books across the country (wink-wink).

Thank you to John Bryan for continuing to keep up my website and converting these books to the proper formats.

Many thanks to the store owners and managers that have agreed to carry my books: Genuine Georgia in Greensboro, Georgia, Lona Gallery in Lawrenceville, The Paisley Bag in Wrens, The Book

Worm in Louisville and The Georgia College and State University campus book store in Milledgeville.

Lastly, thank you as always to my husband and son for their continued patience with my writing.

I love you all and appreciate all of your efforts.

Sincerely,

*T. S. Dawson*

## Disclaimer

Although I do my best to use real landmarks and places in my in my stories, they are just that, stories. There are pieces of me in each and every book I write and people who know me might recognize those pieces. Not one of my books is an autobiography nor are any of them a biography of one of my friends or family members. I write for entertainment purposes. If along the way I parlay a little history of Georgia and its people, that's just a bonus.

Thank you for reading.

With Kind Regards,

*T.S. Dawson*

"The secret of a good memory is attention, and attention to a subject depends on our interest in it. We rarely forget that which has made a deep impression on our minds."--Tryon Edwards

I don't have an excellent memory, but if they gave a quiz on the details of the day my daddy died; it wouldn't even have to be a multiple choice quiz. It could be the kind where you write in the answers in sentence form.

1) What smell was in the air that day?

The windows were up and the neighbor next door had just mowed their yard leaving it smelling like wild onions, dandelions and crabgrass. Yes, fresh cut grass and summer was the smell.

2) What were you wearing?

I was wearing a yellow jumper with white polka-dots and ribbon that tied on top of my shoulders to hold up the top. I also had pigtails with yellow ribbons tied in them. My socks were white. They folded over and had lace. I was such a girly girl back then.

3) What did you have for lunch?

Daddy took me to Michael's, a restaurant where my Granny, his mother, was a waitress and I had a drumstick and mashed potatoes. They had white table cloths and I didn't spill anything. He was so proud of me that he got tears in his eyes.

Those questions and answers could go on for days, but if there was an essay question it might be: Tell in detail how your father died.

"Lucy, be a good girl for Daddy and stay in here until Mommy comes to get you. She'll be here in a few minutes."

Daddy sat me down on the floor of the closet in my bedroom and handed me my favorite doll, Lisa, a Cabbage Patch Kid that Santa had brought me the Christmas before. He kissed the top of my head and the last thing he said to me was, "Please don't ever think any of this is your fault."

I was completely oblivious to what he was talking about. I hadn't spilled or broken anything so I couldn't imagine what might be my fault. My attention span was about as big as a gnat's, so I started twirling Lisa's brown hair in my fingers as he closed the accordion doors to the closet.

I heard Daddy's footsteps on the hardwood floor as he crossed my room. I could also hear the hum of the ceiling fan. There was enough space between the slats to allow light in. I was shut up in the closet, but I wasn't in the dark and I wasn't scared.

I pulled the ribbon out of Lisa's hair and did my best to braid it. The yarn fell apart in my hands each time I tried. I twisted it around and around in clumps, not knowing I had to divide it in three sections and weave it. I didn't have a clue what I was doing, but I was content with playing while I waited for Mama.

Suddenly there was a thud. It was a bouncing thud that reverberated under me and it frightened me. I sat my doll down and laid down flat on the floor so I could see under the door. Peeping under the door I could see one of the kitchen chairs laying on its side, but that was all. I couldn't see Daddy anymore and I couldn't hear him. The entire house was dreadfully silent except for the sound of the ceiling fan. It wasn't humming anymore.

"Ggggrrrrrggghhhh." The fan struggled and growled with a loud and steady groan. There wasn't even that tick that the pull cords of the light and the fan usually made when clinking together as the blades spun. I didn't hear Daddy leave, but the sense of being alone overcame me. The hair stood up on the back of my neck. I grabbed Lisa and held her tight for comfort.

I started with a whisper, "Daddy?"

I got no response and the more frightened I became the louder I called for him. The whisper quickly escalated to screams that strained my throat and tears streaked my face. I had never been left alone before and I couldn't understand what was going on. I knew better than to disobey Daddy so I stayed put and squeezed Lisa tighter and cried.

The back door to our house flew open and Mama came running. Over the sound of the grinding fan, I could hear her heels thump against the floor as she ran through the house screaming my name. I pulled myself out of the fit of calling for Daddy and screamed, "Mama!"

Our house was tiny so it was only a matter of seconds before Mama was in the doorway of my room. Mama let out a blood curdling scream that rang my ears and sent me back into full blown hysterics calling for her. She didn't waste a moment.

"Cover your eyes, Lucy." Mama said as calmly as she could before opening the closet door.

I did as she asked and she scooped me up. She did her best to bury my face in her shoulder as she ran with me from the room and the house and out into the front yard. But I saw him. His arms were limp, flopped down by his sides, and the toes of his shoes pointed down. His eyes bulged open. I saw why the fan was straining. The blades couldn't turn for the rope.

The thing about the quiz that I didn't think I would ever get right was the bonus question. That question was why. Why did he do it?

Mama tried to tell me he fell trying to fix the fan, but I knew that wasn't true. I think I knew better but I never knew why. It wasn't something Mama allowed me to talk about. If it wasn't my fault, whose was it and why would he do such a thing? I was always interested in this answer. There was hardly a day that passed that I didn't wonder.

Chapter 1

"Lucy, it's hotter than four Hells!" Mama griped as she held her arms up in front of the box fan to get a little relief from the pouring sweat.

That summer, Thomson, Georgia was just that hot. It was sweltering, sticky and humid. It was Georgia weather, and just because it was typical didn't make anyone like it any better.

It was the first Sunday after the school year had ended and I was kicked back on the couch reading one of Mama's old Nancy Drew books. My mind flipped back and forth between the words on the page and thoughts of how my summer normally went. That was all changing this year, and I wasn't sure how I felt about it. If emotions were broken down into mathematical equations, excitement plus dread equaled nervousness.

Normally, I stayed with my Nanny, my mother's mother, in the summers while Mama worked. Nanny's house was the one place hotter than ours. We had one air conditioner that Mama only turned on at night. Nanny didn't even have that, but I didn't care. Nothing bothered me at Nanny's house.

My days with Nanny were spent picking peas, corn and tomatoes, and when we weren't picking, we were shelling, shucking or stewing. I thought those things were fun and that everyone did them. That showed how much I knew.

My luck staying at Nanny's during the summer ran out this year. This summer the attorney my mother worked for wrangled a job for me at the kennel of the fox hunting club where he was a member. Yep, the summer of 1996 was the summer I got my first job.

I was never privileged enough to go to the fox hunting club before. I knew where it was, but I had never been lucky enough to make it through the front gate. We had ridden by it a number of times and I had seen the men in the red coats on the horses out by the Washington Highway with all of the hounds scurrying around. Seeing them from the road was as close as I had ever come. The Wrightsboro Fox Hunting Club was mostly a place for the private school kids and I was definitely not one of those.

My first day on the job there I was pleased as punch. Mama drove me out there early in the morning before she went to work. I was excited as we turned down the driveway and drove past the stable. I decided to leave dread at home that morning.

I was in awe of the place; mouth dropped open, eyes popping out. It wasn't even 8:00 a.m. and there were people buzzing about with their horses at the stable as we passed by. Everyone there looked pretty, even the men. I wasn't sure how, but I'd been

11

magically teleported into the pages of a magazine and was stepping through an ad for Polo cologne.

This was a new adventure for me and it was quite the saving grace from the heat. The kennel at the fox hunting club had industrial sized oscillating fans. It didn't take much to impress me. I mean, it wasn't real air conditioning, but it beat the snot out of the box fans and the wobbly ceiling fans we had at home. I quickly realized that the other half's hunting dogs lived more comfortably than me and half of my family. I tried my best to shrug off the thoughts that made me feel small and to ignore the growing feeling that I was nothing more than the hired help.

By my third day on the job it was no longer an adventure. I missed Nanny and the fun I had with her. I didn't dare complain about the kennel and I didn't dare beg to go back to Nanny's. Mama was skilled in the art of shaming me into guilt for being ungrateful so I knew better than to breathe a word. I came to the strange conclusion that I was ready to forget summer altogether and go back to school. I typically liked school about as much as normal folks liked splinters.

Mama was the office manager for a local attorney. Of course he wasn't the one that represented James Brown so I never heard his name on the evening news. I heard it enough at home though. "Mr. Watson" this and "Mr. Watson" that, Mama would go on and on. He was the authority on everything and every now and then she would slip up and refer to him by his first name, Boyd.

Mr. Boyd Watson, some relation to one of the prominent families in town, had been my benefactor for about as long as I could remember. Mr. Watson had a daughter of his own. So other than feeling sorry for me because he paid my mama chicken feed or because I had no father, I'm not sure what his motives were.

Mr. Watson seemed like a nice man and Mama was very fond of him. I mean, he paid for my dance lessons from the time I was six. He also afforded me the luxury of piano lessons until my teacher explained to Mama that it was a complete waste of money. I was about as musically inclined as a concrete brick, I believe those were her exact words. It was of no help that I didn't have a piano to practice on at home. Our tiny match box house on Dixie Drive didn't have a wall big enough to accommodate one.

On my fourth day at the kennel, I had more than my fair share of barking dogs, annoying flies and stinking dog poop. On day five, I had to help birth a litter of puppies. As I cleaned each squirming wet pup with my bare hands, I came to the conclusion that I no longer adored puppies. That chore was more disgusting than finding one of those awful fat worms in a ripe tomato. Most folks called them dogs, but to the members of the hunt they were "hounds". No matter what you called them, I was sour on the whole lot of them.

"Quittin' time!" yelled Dwayne, the kennel foreman, when the time clock struck 5:00 p.m. on Friday afternoon. Well, he wasn't really the foreman, but that was sure how he introduced himself when I met him on Monday.

I was spraying down one of the stalls at the far end of the building, but I heard him. In a huff under my breath, I mocked him, "Quittin' time. If only..."

Mrs. Francine Pope worked at the kennel too. She was a member, but also in charge of the place. She was the real foreman, and she was usually out on the property with one group of hounds or another. Most of the time it was just me and Dwayne left there alone to tend to the rest of the dogs.

Although Dwayne was older than I was, I knew quite well who he was. Thomson was not as small as Warrenton or Dearing, but it was still small enough that most everyone knew everyone else, if only by reputation.

And Dwayne had himself a reputation. It was a bit scandalous. He and some cousins of his got bored one summer and decided to invent another way to play mailbox baseball. Instead of taking baseball bats to the mailboxes like normal country boys, they went to the local Gurley's grocery store and bought household cleaning supplies and made bombs.

They put their homemade bombs in the mailboxes and watched them explode. It was all over the pages of <u>The McDuffie Progress</u>, and at least one episode of the nightly news on Channel 6. The FBI was called in because once a mailbox is put out by the road it becomes federal property. It was a real big to-do at the time and the only reason Dwayne didn't serve some time was because he was the youngest of the group and because they figured he suffered enough when he blew two fingers off of his right hand while arming one of the bombs. Ultimately, the word in the paper was that the FBI didn't know whether the boys were too smart for their own good or too stupid to know better.

Financially, Dwayne's family was one of the bottom rung families that sent their kid to private school. Hiring an attorney, Mr. Watson, and keeping Dwayne from serving time at YDC took all of the money they typically spent on his education. With the money gone, Dwayne was sent to the public school with the rest of us and that's where he had graduated last Friday night. Most of those that graduated with him were off on their senior trip, but not Dwayne. He was here spraying down stalls and birthing puppies with me.

Due to his hand being the way it was, the kids at our school made fun of Dwayne. I wasn't one of the ones that made fun of him. We didn't talk about it in the few days that I was there. He seemed like a bit of an outcast and I don't think he had many friends. He worked hard at the kennel and, unlike me, he seemed to enjoy it. This was his fourth summer there. He'd been there since he was fourteen.

I liked Dwayne just fine, but I hated the kennel and I hated Mr. Boyd Watson. All of his kindness toward me was forgotten and I was convinced he hated me too. I was also convinced he needed to mind his own business and not do me any more favors.

My weekend whizzed by so fast it was a blur. The only thing worth remembering was that Mama replaced the ceiling fan in my bedroom. It had been original to the house and sounded like it too. For so many years, it made the most God-awful racket. I knew damn well why it made the noise and I also knew that Mama probably would have changed it out years ago if only I had let her. Well, Mama didn't replace it herself. The handy man that Mr. Watson sent over replaced it. The room now had a strange new rhythm. I still heard the sound of crickets and the random barking of the neighbor's dog through the open screened window, but the constant beat made by the off-kilter fan was gone and replaced by a low hum. The fan was just one more thing Mr. Watson had repaired that I didn't necessarily believe needed to be fixed.

Monday morning arrived and Mama had to threaten to get me out of bed. I wasn't five any more so the promise of ice cream at the end of the week no longer worked.

"I won't let you go to the movies Friday night if you aren't dressed and at the breakfast table in five minutes," she shouted from the kitchen.

That worked. I rolled out of bed and dressed in record time. Only a real social misfit would not be at the movie theater on Friday night. It was where all of the teenagers hung out that weren't of driving age. Our mothers would drop us off and pick us up after the movie. If you were one of the few that were allowed to date before you were able to drive, it meant the boy's mother did the dropping off and picking up. This was the second summer that I was allowed to go to the movies, but I was not one of the fortunate few who were allowed to date yet.

On the ride to work I thought about the trip to the movies this past Friday night. I sat next to Maggie McCorkle on one side and Kevin McCorkle, Maggie's cousin, on the other. We saw a movie called The Phantom. I could hardly watch the movie for squirming to keep Kevin from trying to hold my hand or worse, put his hand on my inner thigh or around my shoulders to cop a feel. I begged Maggie to trade seats with me, but she refused. She was content playing scared and cuddling up to my cousin Thomas on her other side. We weren't allowed to date, but nothing was said about us not being able to bring our cousins with us. No one had to know we traded cousins once we got to the theater. Unfortunately, Kevin was from the grade below us and it was definitely not a fair trade.

There were some technical difficulties with the projector at the theater and the movie ran late. What I saw of the movie was alright, but the best part of the night was when I was standing on the curb waiting for Mama to pick me up. I was afraid Mama would be waiting outside, but as it turns out she was late too. I had a feeling she went to Mr. Watson's house while I was at the movies, but she'd never tell.

Maggie and Kevin got picked up first and Thomas caught a ride with them. The crowd had dwindled and I was one of about five left waiting. It was cooler than usual and the street was buzzing back and forth with the older teens cruising from the Sonic parking lot on Hill Street to the McDonalds out by the interstate and back. I could hardly wait to be one of them.

A streetlight on the opposite side of the road flickered and it held my attention until traffic backed up from the light and I noticed a guy in a navy blue Ford Bronco. It was one of the big ones with the top and the doors taken off. He never saw me looking at him, but boy how I looked. I could hear the music from his radio playing "Black" by Pearl Jam and he was singing along. I never saw all of his face, only the side and the back of his head. He had sandy blond hair. He was tapping his foot on the floor board and strumming his hand on the steering wheel as he sang along. From what I could see of him, he looked like someone I would have seen in <u>Tiger Beat</u>

or <u>Teen Beat</u>. Yeah, I could have cut out his poster and hung it on my wall any day of the week.

That song played and I fantasized about being in the passenger seat and singing along. That's the kind of guy I wanted, not some measly freckled face boy that was fresh out of middle school. No, Kevin McCorkle would never do for me. I wondered what it would be like to have a boyfriend like Mr. Ford (the silly name I quickly gave him). Heck, I wondered what it would be liked to have any boyfriend.

"Spinning" was a word that was repeated in the song and the music made me feel like twirling. I became a Pearl Jam fan for life in that one instant. I lost myself and I lived a thousand fantasies in the span of only the precious few seconds Mr. Ford was stopped at that light. I would have lived at least a thousand more if Mama hadn't started honking the horn. She was about eight cars behind him toward the railroad tracks.

Thoughts of Mr. Ford carried me the rest of the weekend. That, and a copy of the Ten CD. Monday at the kennel was pretty typical. First we checked the hounds for ticks from the Saturday morning hunt. After that lovely scavenger hunt, we hosed down the stalls, and then came the feeding. I was elbow deep in a bucket of chicken necks, and just as I started to sling out a heavy handful, Dwayne called my name.

The incessant barking made it hard to hear him the first time, but the second time he screamed a bit louder and a full sentence. "Lucy, you have a visitor!"

"Who in the world is here to see me?" There was no need saying it under my breath, he couldn't hear me. I said it in my full speaking voice.

I took the bucket with me to keep the dogs from tearing down the stall door to get at it and started walking toward Dwayne who was standing at the doorway at the far end of the building. As I passed Dwayne, he took the bucket from me and started throwing out the chicken to the dogs in the stall closest to him.

For a split second, I forgot about the missing fingers and just noticed Dwayne's face. He wasn't hard to look at; rusty brown hair and brown eyes, a few freckles over the bridge of his nose. He was eighteen and I was a month away from being sixteen. Sure, he'd already graduated high school and I was going into my sophomore year, but Papa was three years older than Nanny. I had never had a summer romance before and since I'd probably never see Mr. Ford again, I might as well forget about him. No sooner had the notion of a romance with Dwayne barely entered my head when a cold shiver suddenly ran over me and I snapped out of that daydream. There were much better dreams to have, and there was no shaking the image of Mr. Ford or the sound of Eddie Vedder's voice echoing that one word. Spinning. Dwayne would never send me spinning.

"I'm not expecting anyone," I explained to Dwayne as I washed my hands at the dog wash station. "Who is it?"

"Lily Watson."

"What does she want?"

"I don't know." Dwayne shrugged. "They don't tell me anything. I'm just the help around here."

I shrugged back and headed out the door.

I hadn't been outside since I arrived that morning. The inside the kennel was lit with florescent tube bulbs and those really wore on my eyes. That being the case, when I stepped outside I was temporarily blinded by the sunlight. It was beating down and I raised my hand to shield my eyes. As I brought my hand to my face, I realized it still smelled like raw chicken. In my blindness, I wondered if my sense of smell was just heightened. Surely I didn't smell like rotting chicken and dog crap. As I fretted over the possibility of embarrassment, it was quickly affirmed by my visitor.

"Wow! You stink!" I recognized the voice. It was definitely Lily. From what I could see of her, she was fanning her nose. "Daddy said you were working out here this summer."

"Yeah, my first job," I sighed.

There was a long pause before Lily spoke again. "I envy you. Daddy's never let me have a job."

"Excuse me?" I turned my head to keep her from seeing me roll my eyes.

I couldn't understand why anyone would envy me working in the kennel. She could smell me and yet she still made that statement. I was terribly confused.

"I envy that you get to get out of the house and that you get to make your own money." Lily dabbed the sweat from her brow with a paper towel that she took out of her pocket. I had sweat all over me and it would have taken a whole roll of paper towels to dab me off.

I held back my snarky comment of "what makes me so special?" I didn't ask because it wasn't that I was special at all. It was Lily that was special. She never worked a day in her life and she'd never have to. He didn't keep her from working because they were so rich that she didn't need to. He kept her from having a job because she was so frail and sickly.

I had known Lily for as long as I could remember. She was five years older than I was and she had leukemia. The sinister disease operated like a Jack in the Box. Just when you least expected, it popped its ugly head out and scared the wits out of everyone. The leukemia had taken a toll on Lily and Mr. Watson, just in different ways.

What was left of Lily's hair was the color of mine, brown with a few red highlights and it had a natural curl like mine. She was the kind of rake thin that made her look like the concentration camp survivors we learned about in world history. If she weighed ninety pounds soaking wet, it would be a miracle.

Most people would be bitter, but she wasn't. The statement about envying me because I was allowed to work was the closest thing to anything nasty I had ever heard her say and it was only nasty due to my own perception.

Until I entered kindergarten, she was my best friend. Nanny still worked at the time so Mama left me with Lily and Molly, the woman that tutored Lily when she wasn't well enough to go to the private school. When she was in remission, we played together. The main thing I remembered playing with her was school. She was the teacher and I shared the role of student with a bunch of stuffed animals.

I believe Lily always wanted to be a teacher. She graduated high school two years ago, but the leukemia flared back up. They didn't think she was going to make it that time and I suppose they just never saw the point in enrolling her in college.

"I hope you don't mind me interrupting you at work." Lily leaned against the tree outside of the kennel door for better balance.

Lily's legs weren't at all like the legs of a normal twenty year old. They were little more than bones with what appeared to be hubcaps for knees. If my legs looked like that I would probably never wear a dress, but Lily had always been braver than I was and she had on a cotton sundress. I think it was pink, but in the blinding sun I wasn't real sure. If I had been through what she'd been through, I would have given up years ago.

"No, that's fine. I needed a break from the barking." I turned my head one time too many when speaking and smelled myself again. "I'm sorry, I smell."

"You do smell and you'll want to do something about that before your riding lesson on Wednesday."

"Riding lesson?"

"Blueberry is back from the vet in Wrens and someone needs to ride him so I signed you up for riding lessons."

Blueberry was Lily's horse. I had always wanted a horse and a piano, but we didn't have space or money for either.

"Are you sure you want me riding him?"

Lily shook her head. "Do you know someone else who's already out here and I trust enough to allow them to borrow my horse?"

Before I could answer, Lily repeated herself. "Riding lessons on Wednesday afternoon before they take the hounds out for the hunt. The guy will be around for you. You might want to find a way to get the smell of death off you between now and then. I gotta go. Molly's waiting in the car to drive me home." She glanced in the direction of the idling automobile.

"Okay. Thanks."

Lily steadied herself, taking back her weight from against the tree trunk. Once she was on her feet good, she looked me over one more time.

"I guess I can't call you my little sister anymore." That's what she used to call me, her little sister.

"Why's that?" I asked.

"You've grown a foot since the last time I saw you. You aren't little anymore."

Lily smiled sweetly at me and the skin on her cheeks stretched over her bones. I was reminded that she wasn't much more than a skeleton and I felt so bad for her. We had both stopped growing and I was about six inches taller than she was. All of the drugs and treatments and the disease itself, had likely stunted her growth. I don't think Lily was even five feet tall.

"I'll always be your little sister." I leaned over and offered her my hand. "Let me help you."

We were both only children so when we played together when we were little, we would pretend that we were sisters. Even though she held onto my hand, Lily staggered away toward the waiting pink Cadillac that Molly drove. It was a real Mary Kay car that Molly had earned selling cosmetics on the side. I felt terrible for my attitude earlier about Lily envying me. I think she might have been the true definition of poor little rich girl.

Chapter 2

The next morning I arrived at work the same as all of the days before. The morning was going as usual when the phone rang. It was for me and Dwayne looked awful put out that I was getting calls at work.

"Hello?" I answered.

"Lucy, it's Lily. Edward is going to come by this morning."

"Who's Edward?"

"The guy from the stable that's going to give you riding lessons."

I had been kept so busy in the kennel that I hadn't met anyone that worked at the stables yet.

Lily went on, "Don't say anything, but Dwayne called Daddy and told him he couldn't spare you for lessons."

"What?" I had only casually mentioned the lessons to Dwayne.

"He told Daddy he couldn't spare you. Daddy said and I quote, 'That's funny since you didn't want a girl in what you called your kennel.' Daddy gets what Daddy wants and evidently he wants you to have riding lessons too so he set Dwayne straight. I'd watch what I said to him if I were you."

I glanced Dwayne's way as I listened to Lily's warning. Dwayne was watching me. Before I thought it was harmless, but now it gave me the creeps.

"Thanks for looking out for me."

It wasn't that her Daddy wanted to get what he wanted. He always made sure Lily got what she wanted and since Lily wanted me to have riding lessons that meant Mr. Watson wanted me to have riding lessons.

"Call me after the lesson and let me know how it went. Also, don't get any ideas about Edward. He's too old for you."

I completely turned my back to Dwayne and did my best to keep him from hearing me tease Lily. "What do you know about older men and having ideas?"

"Never-you-mind about that. Now, get back to work."

Lily and I said our goodbyes and no sooner did I hang up the phone than did Dwayne want to know every word of the conversation.

"Oh, no, it was nothing. Just Lily being Lily."

Dwayne pressed a bit more, but I didn't budge on my answer.

"Alright." Dwayne rolled his eyes.

Of course he knew I wasn't telling him everything, but thanks to Lily's warning, I wasn't about to. Since I wasn't forthcoming, he put me on the dirtiest job he could think of. He explained that I had to express the dogs' anal glands. Dwayne showed me how it was done and then picked the most rambunctious dogs in the place and put them in a stall for me.

"What are you doing?" A loud voice came from behind me.

Before I could whip my head around to see who it was, the question was then redirected at Dwayne. "What is she doing?"

I scrambled to get up from down on all fours where I had been wrestling with the hound.

"She's expressing their anal glands?" Dwayne's tone was that of smirking authority, but it didn't match the other male voice.

The dogs were still pouncing all over me, but I got to my feet. No introduction was needed. From Lily's statement, I understood exactly why she said that to me about not getting any ideas. That must have been Edward, the trainer she spoke of.

"Did he tell you to do that?" He turned toward me and I felt my cheeks flush as I got a frontal view of him.

My mind was cluttered with the word "Wow!" and my heart literally skipped a beat. I couldn't open my mouth for fear of drooling or stuttering or something equally embarrassing. All I could do was nod my head.

"Why on Earth would you make her do that? Those dogs are about as big as she is and they're damn near wild."

Dwayne walked up to him and bowed up. "Why don't you stick to running the stables and leave me to my kennel."

"Your kennel? We'll see about that."

"Yeah, we will! You'll be back in Virginia and I'll be right here doing what I do in *my* kennel." Dwayne emphasized the word, "my".

I was a little nervous that they were going to come to blows. Dwayne was scrappy, but my money was on Edward and I didn't even know him. I guess I didn't need to know him to know that I wanted Dwayne taught a lesson about messing with me.

Edward was dressed in riding attire with the boots, the tan stretch pants, white polo shirt and his hair was still damp like he had just gotten out of the shower. He towered over Dwayne by at least six inches.

Dwayne was dressed in work boots, jeans and a t-shirt, same as me, except my jeans were cut off shorts. The notion that I might have been attracted to Dwayne the day before was a long gone thing of the past. All of his stolen glances at me now seemed a little perverted.

"Miss Lucy," Edward called me, "I'm supposed to give you riding lessons this morning. Are you ready?"

I looked at Dwayne. I was almost afraid to leave as I understood that I had to come back later. Who knew what would happen then?

"Come on. Mr. Watson's already paid me and you don't want me to tell him you wasted his money." Edward held open the gate for me and, with the heel of his boot, pushed back the hounds so I could get out. Edward didn't kick them like I'd seen Dwayne do. He just gave them a shove. I had stayed in the fenced-in stall while they had words. I figured I was safer in there with the dogs than I was out there with the two of them.

Dwayne huffed and turned and went to the office while I followed Edward outside.

Between the kennel and the stable, I made one giant mental note as to Edward's backside. I tried not to look, but I couldn't help myself. It was about fifty yards between the two buildings and I spent most of the walk staring at my own feet, but he really was a magnet for my eyes. Halfway across the yard Edward looked back over his shoulder and I thought surely I was busted. I diverted my eyes as he off handedly introduced himself.

"By the way, I'm Edward. Edward Stephens."

Although he already knew my name, I said it anyway, "I'm Lucy Meeks."

"Right."

For all the regard there was in the word, "right", I might as well have said my name was Seymour Butts. As I saw it now, Lily needn't have bothered with her advice about Edward. He was fun to look at, definitely older than me and clearly out of my league. This notion was further cemented in my brain once we reached the stable.

The stable was yet another eye opener about the way rich people kept their animals. The hounds had pretty dang close to air conditioning and, although they were called stalls too, each horse had a room that was bigger than my bedroom.

The smell of the stable was a far cry from that of the kennel. The kennel was the awful combination of wet dog and poop. As soon as we crested the threshold of the opening at the end of the stable the scent of hay began to mix with that of fresh cut grass, oats and leather. There wasn't even a trace of horse manure in the air at all.

To the far end Edward marched and I continued to follow five paces behind him. We passed countless stalls before we came to the one where Blueberry was waiting. I knew it was Blueberry only because I noticed his name written in chalk on the door of the stall when Edward stepped through it. I stood outside, taking in my surroundings. Blueberry's stall was the third from the end on the right hand side of the building.

"Are you waiting on an engraved invitation before you come in here?"

"No," I replied, barely above a whisper and went inside. I was about as useful inside the stall as I was outside.

"Excuse me."

Edward squeezed past me and took the saddle from on top the stall door and slung it over Blueberry's back. I felt the breeze and a stronger smell of oiled leather, like my softball glove, as it flew past me.

Again, I found myself trying not to look at him, but I couldn't help but notice his arms while he worked with the saddle. He was tan and freckled and made Dwayne look like a shrimp. I could see his muscles flex above his elbows as he pulled at the belt to tighten the saddle under Blueberry's belly.

Edward did most of the work in silence. That silence was broken when he asked if I had ever saddled a horse before. He simply shook his head in disgust at my answer. Our silence was broken again rather abruptly when Whitney Knox popped in.

"Well, well, well, Edward, Edward, Edward."

Whitney flirted and all but licked his neck and groped him right in front of me. It was as if I wasn't there at all.

"There's no place like home," I clicked the heels of my boots together and said that three times as I stroked Blueberry's nose.

From the corner of my eye I saw her glare at me. Miss Private School let go of Edward only to acknowledge my presence.

"Don't you work in the kennel?" Blueberry let out a good roll of his lips and puff of air, but I heard what Whitney said and I understood the translation. I had the unfortunate pleasure of knowing Whitney Knox most all of my life. If I was Laura Ingalls, she was most certainly my Nelly Olsen, right down to the blonde hair and curls.

Ever since we were children, Whitney had a way of making me feel insignificant and letting me know I did not belong in her atmosphere. As always, she was letting me know that again. I was embarrassed and reminded of how I despised Mr. Boyd Watson. If only he had left me alone I would be safe in my comfort zone at Nanny's. I looked at my watch. Yeah, we would have been ready to watch the first of our morning game shows.

Edward whipped Whitney around and without her really realizing it he saved me and kicked her out of the stall. "Whitney, if you don't mind, I'll catch up with you later." As soon as Whitney had been sent on her way, Edward went back to saddling up Blueberry.

"Is there anything I can do to help?" I moved to let down one of the stirrups that had gotten caught on the horn of the saddle.

Before I could touch the stirrup, came another chastising. "You can go wash your hands from handling the dogs."

Edward sounded stern and I immediately started toward the opening of the stall. Everything at the kennel had happened so fast and this was another embarrassment compounded on top of the others.

I turned around just outside of the stall and went back. "I'm going to go wash my hands, but we really don't have to do this. I won't tell you didn't give me lessons. You can keep whatever Mr. Watson paid you."

Tears were on their way. I could feel them coming. I wiped one eye and then the other. "I've had enough of being put in my place for one day."

I said my peace and started to walk away. Hardly three paces through the stable Edward caught up to me. He grabbed me by the arm and pulled me back into Blueberry's stall. I really didn't know what was going on. I gasped and tried to jerk away from him, but his grip on me was pretty firm. The proximity to him was both startling and exhilarating.

"First of all," he started in a voice indicative of not wanting the rest of the barn to hear while he came into my personal space at the same time. "If you knew me at all, you would know that I would never keep money that I didn't earn and I won't go along with a lie. Secondly, don't think for one second that girl's better than you. She's cut her eye-teeth on half the boys in town and it doesn't take a rocket scientist to see that. Thirdly, and listen closely, don't ever let that douche back at the kennel make you do something that could get you hurt. Don't ever let him belittle you."

"But I didn't know..."

"If there's something you don't know or something that you're unsure of, you come ask me. Do you understand?"

34

I almost said, "Yes, sir," when I answered, but I managed to squeak out a simple "yes". I could hardly think. I didn't know what to make of his speech. He was breathtaking.

Edward backed up from me and took Blueberry by the reigns. "Good. Now suck it up and go wash your hands. When you come back we'll get you up on him."

Despite the drama of the morning, my first riding lesson went well. First of all I didn't fall off the horse and that was a plus. Secondly, I learned how to do what Edward called "posting".

Out in the front pasture by the road, Edward held Blueberry on a long lead. Edward was the sun and Blueberry was the lone planet orbiting around him. I was the sole inhabitant of that planet.

"Bend your knees and keep your weight in your heels!" Edward shook his head. This was my first time on a horse and it was evident.

Blueberry took a few more steps and I did my best to follow Edward's directions.

"Move with your thighs and hips...Heels down!" He had to shout for me to hear him over the horse's hooves.

I bit my lip and concentrated on pulling my toes up in the stirrups to keep my heels down while trying to stand.

"Straighten your back. The object is to keep your behind from touching the saddle."

Edward made a sucking sound through his teeth. Two sharp and high pitched whistles and Blueberry picked up some speed. "Sit when you canter. Post when you trot."

My backside made contact with the saddle seat a couple of times and I was the receiver of some teeth clenching blows. No further explanation was needed as to why I shouldn't touch the seat.

Around we continued, Blueberry and I, with Edward watching all the while. I tried not to look at him, but I could see him from the corner of my eye. I shook off the urge to get more than a sideways glance. The confidence he exuded amazed me.

I tried to count, like an eight count in music, to get with the beat. I counted the strikes of the horse's shoes to the ground. Each time Edward spoke it threw me off my count a little.

"Stop talking!" I huffed under my breath, half wanting him to hear me and half not.

"Don't grip the reigns. Just hold them." Edward scolded me and I rolled my eyes. I was using my arms in tandem with my heels and hips to get me up and down and keep me off the saddle.

"A little tug left or right for direction is all he needs." Edward added.

Blueberry continued in the circle and I gave up the use of my arms. "Five, six, seven, eight," I went on in my head with each step.

Up and down we went and a few more collisions between my butt and the saddle were quite the incentive for me to find a rhythm and stick with it.

I had been told all my life that I was a natural athlete. I danced and played softball and those things came easy to me. I realized it was only my first lesson, but I didn't expect it to be this hard. I was having to contort by body in ways that made me almost want to cry. Blueberry suddenly swung his tail and swatted at a fly. That almost broke my rhythm, but not quite. I was determined to focus and get this right.

After a few minutes Edward shouted. "That's it! That's it! Good! Good!"

In all my days at the kennel, no one had praised me for a good job so this was a nice change.

I smiled as big as I ever had. I was in the middle of thinking, "I've got it," and Edward was saying as much, but I took my eyes off of Blueberry and looked his way only for a split second. Looking at him was a mistake, a big mistake. I lost my balance and suffered the most jarring of impacts. I had never been kicked by a horse before, but I couldn't imagine a swift hoof in the ass to have been much harder.

There were tears in my eyes. "Whoa!!!" I screamed in pain and reared back on the reigns. Blueberry screeched to a halt. I hadn't caught my breath yet when he vaulted me forward. Out of the stirrups I went. If I hadn't grabbed a hold around his neck I would have gone over. I didn't fall off, but I came incredibly close.

Edward came running, "Are you alright?"

I just moaned a little. Modesty kept me from saying what was wrong.

"Your butt hurts?" he asked.

My modesty was gone. I had never had anyone, let alone a virtual stranger, inquire as to the status of my behind before. I turned my face away from him and hugged the opposite side of Blueberry's neck as I tried to slide back into the saddle. I wanted to rub where it hurt, but I didn't dare, not in front of him.

"It's okay. It happens to everyone, but you'll get the hang of it." Edward guided my foot on that side back in to the stirrup.

"It doesn't always hurt like this, does it?" I managed to get the words out.

"No. Practice makes better." Edward winked at me as he caught Blueberry by the strap going to his bit. "Come on, I think you've had enough for today."

We started back toward the stable. It felt like the longest walk or ride of my life. About halfway across Edward brought Blueberry to a stop. He patted his nose and ran his hand from his ears down his mane before looking up to me.

"Remember what I said about the kennel. Don't do anything that you don't feel comfortable with and, if you have a question about something, come find me. And, next week, wear jeans and a pair of real riding boots. Okay?"

I nodded. "Okay."

I had jeans, but I didn't have riding boots. I didn't know what I would do about that, but I would figure it out. For whatever reason, I wanted to please Edward. I promised myself I would beg, borrow or even steal some riding boots and then I would master posting if it killed me.

Edward turned back around and he and Blueberry started to walk again. Once at the stable, Edward offered a hand to help me down. It hadn't occurred to me until my feet hit the ground, there was something off with my right knee. I had been so distracted with the wounds to my pride and my derriere that I hadn't noticed my knee at all. When I did notice it, it made me completely forget about everything else.

Bearing weight on the knee was a challenge. How did I not notice before? I winced and shifted to my left leg and grabbed Edward's arm to steady myself. Lily's words rang in my ears again. I let go as if I'd touched a hot stove. It was hard not to get ideas just standing next to him, let alone touching his firm and muscular arm.

Edward didn't need to be the most observant person in the world. He easily noticed I was having trouble. "Are your knees hurting?"

"Just the right one, but it's nothing." I tried to put weight on it and winced again. This time I played it off by leaning into Blueberry and rubbing his nose.

"Okay, but if one knee hurts and the other doesn't it means I didn't get the stirrups even. You have to tell me these things."

"How can I tell you what I don't know? If that's the only way I've ever known then how am I to know it's not right?" I must have sounded stupid, but I wasn't just talking about my knee. What he said about Dwayne played into my question as well.

"Point taken." Edward handed me the brush from the tack bucket that hung outside of Blueberry's stall. He took one for himself too.

Edward nuzzled Blueberry and stroked his nose, caressing him and preparing him for the touch of the brush. After a few seconds he started brushing Blueberry's mane. I had never brushed a horse before so I waited. I watched him for a moment and then picked a spot on Blueberry and started.

"You know," he looked over Blueberry's back while he brushed. "My sisters say they get this feeling when something's not quite right. I overheard my older sister explaining to the younger once that she just had to trust that feeling. Do you ever get a feeling like that?"

I stopped brushing and looked up at him. I had to think about it.

"Yeah," I started brushing again. "Sometimes."

"I think you need to trust that feeling."

It was obvious we weren't talking about the stirrups anymore. "You really don't like Dwayne, do you?"

"He just rubs me the wrong way." The way Edward didn't make eye contact when he spoke made me think there was more to it than was he was letting on.

"Why?"

"He just does. It's you women that have the intuition."

"Sounds like you have some intuition of your own."

"Nah." He bent over to brush Blueberry's belly. "I don't think that's it."

I leaned under so I could see him all the while continuing to keep my weight on my left leg. The least little bit of pressure on my right and the throbbing pain was just too much. "I'm not so sure. Maybe it's just competing testosterone levels. That's what my mama would say."

"Sounds like your mama's a smart lady."

Blueberry's coat was soft as any blanket I had ever felt and just as warm. He had a tinge of sweat over his back from where the saddle had been. The shine of his dark hair lying flat against his enormous body fascinated me. Today was the first time I had really seen a horse this close up. They really are beautiful creatures and I was learning that first hand now. It almost seemed like another daydream.

Edward had moved on toward the hindquarters and was still brushing. I went forward as he went back. Blueberry was a chestnut colored horse with a white stripe down his nose that resembled a cross. I couldn't resist the urge to press my cheek to the bridge of his nose, to lay my head against that white streak. I brushed one side of his face with one hand and petted him down the other.

The little bit of pressure applied by my forehead to his nose was enough to take the burden off of my knee and allowed me to balance on my good leg. I tried not to focus on the pain. Of course there were all sorts of complaints from the knee to my brain, but those thoughts were clouded by remembrances of the thrilling ride and how relaxing it was now to just to be in the company of this amazing creature.

By the time Edward and I finished brushing I could hardly stand. I continued to try my best to hide how bad it really was. But the fact that I was wearing shorts didn't help that cause. My knee was swelling and Edward noticed.

"We should get some ice for that." He gestured toward my knee as he escorted Blueberry into his stall.

"Oh, it's nothing," I shrugged.

"Your right knee is nearly twice the size of the left. I feel terrible. You really should have told me about the stirrups."

"I'll be fine. Don't worry about it."

There were plenty of girls that would have broken down in tears just to guilt him into taking care of them and for no other reason than to spend more time with him. I was not that type of girl. I was the suffer-in-silence type when it came to physical pain. Besides, I was no stranger to a little knee pain. I had been the catcher on the softball team for as long as I had been playing.

"Let me run upstairs and I'll get some ice for you," Edward insisted.

My bravery was beginning to waiver. It was being replaced by my instinct to be what I really was, a teenage girl with a steadily forming crush. Maybe I was one of "those" girls after-all.

There was a bench about three stalls down and back toward the center of the horse barn. "I'll help you over there and then I'll run up to my apartment and get the ice."

Ah, Edward lived in the apartment upstairs. I hadn't known there was an apartment in the top of the barn and I hadn't given any thought to where he might live.

Edward helped me to the bench and then darted off through an opening that led out of the front of the stables. I sat there waiting so long that three different people stopped, noticed my leg and offered to help. I thanked them, but assured them all I was fine. I even told them that Edward had gone to get ice for it.

Ten minutes or more passed before Edward returned with a Ziploc bag of ice in hand. Handing the ice to me, he explained, "I went ahead and called Mr. Watson. At dinner last night he and Lily said that your mother worked for him. I spoke with her..."

I cut him off as he was taking a seat next to me. "You called my mother?" I was mortified. He saw me as a child and he called my mother. I slapped my forehead.

"Well, yes," he continued. "There's no way you can work this afternoon with your knee like that."

"You'd be surprised what I can do on my..."

Edward snickered and I snapped. "What are you laughing at?!!!"

Edward looked away and covered his mouth. He tried to hide the signs of his amusement. "Nothing. You really are green, aren't you?"

I didn't really know what he meant by that so I didn't have an answer. I didn't think it was a yes or no question anyway.

We sat in silence for a few minutes while I held the ice tightly to my knee. I could tell he was still trying not to laugh and, despite the distraction of the ice and the swelling, I was back to trying not to look at him. He was quite possibly the best looking human being I'd ever laid eyes on. Regardless of his looks, there was something about him that kept me from being able to stay mad at him.

"Well, Green," (apparently he'd given me a nickname) "I offered to run you up to the office to your mother and she said that would be fine." He glanced down at my knee. "So whenever you are up for it, we'll get going."

On one hand I wanted to, but on the other, I remembered Dwayne. I thought of him waiting in the kennel for me to come back after my riding lesson. I thought about how he would have to handle all of the afternoon chores by himself. Those thoughts made me giddy inside. It served him right. Dwayne didn't have a nickname for me, but I'm sure he'd have some choice names he called me when I didn't show back up that afternoon.

"I'm ready whenever you are."

Edward stood and offered his hand to help me up. The simmering crush on him made me want to take his hand and never let go. But oddly it was pride that made me reluctantly take his hand.

"You know," I said as he helped me hobble toward the opposite end of the stable, "nothing's broken, it's just sore. I don't understand why it's swelling like this."

"You over worked it that's all. I'll fix the stirrups and this won't happen again. Riding is supposed to be fun, not painful."

I limped a few more steps. "It was fun." I smiled up at him and Edward smiled back. We went out the same end of the stable where we had first entered prior to my lesson. "I'm parked around front," Edward directed and we continued around to the front of the building. "Come on, Green, gimp it on over here."

Chapter 3

Edward had a good hold on me. I gave up limping and I hopped on one foot to do my part more efficiently. I looked ahead of us and my mouth fell open at what I saw. Around the end of the rusty red horse trailer that hadn't budged in all of the days I had been coming to work we continued and on the other side of it was a navy blue Bronco. I instantly recognized it. It was the one I gawked over in front of the movie theater. Navy blue, no top and no doors, it was definitely the same one. I looked to Edward, sandy blonde hair, tan. He was the guy that night, the one I had dreamed about ever since. He was Mr. Ford.

Lily's words of warning were now falling squarely on deaf ears. I had spent the better part of my morning trying not to look at Edward, but I hadn't succeeded until now. Now, I couldn't look at him for fear of him noticing the rosiness of my cheeks, the embarrassment written all over me, the crush I had on him since well before that morning.

We sped out of the driveway from the hunt club property onto the paved road. The top was still down and the knobby tires made a racket of road noise and between that and the radio blaring, I couldn't hear a word Edward said to me.

"What did you say? I can't hear you." I brushed back my hair, which was blowing every which direction, but didn't turn toward him. I kept watch of the ditch along my side of the road as we sped along.

Nearly screaming, he asked, "How old are you?"

"I'll be sixteen in two weeks." I yelled over the roar around me.

"Ah."

That's when I turned back to him. "'Ah,' what does that mean?"

"Nothing." He raised the corner of his mouth.

"Seriously?"

"I thought you were younger." Edward took his eyes off of the road ahead and smiled at me for a split second.

"Really? Why?" I was puzzled. I never thought about it much and I never cared how old I looked until now. Now I only cared because I knew he was older, but I didn't know how much older.

"I guess because you are tiny."

"I'm not that tiny. Honestly, with that way of thinking it would mean you must be old. I mean, you're tall and, well, uh...real old." I turned my head and went back to looking at the ditch.

Edward laughed, "I'm not that old."

Of course that begged the question, "How old are you then?"

"Nineteen, almost twenty, but not as close to twenty as you are to sixteen."

Instead of staying straight, Edward made the turn onto the road that ran next to Dudley nursery

47

and headed toward the Lincolnton highway. That road wasn't laid with asphalt as the one the hunt club was on. This one was a mix of gravel and concrete and it made a world of racket with the tires slapping and jolting over it. It felt as if we bounced from one end of the road all the way to the other and all the while the music blared, not Pearl Jam this time, but something similar. I didn't like it as much.

"If I keep listening to this, I'll have to call that suicide hotline that MTV promotes all the time."

The radio was the most modern thing about the Bronco. It was a Pioneer pull out CD player. Edward reached over and messed with it. The next song up was a little less angst filled.

"Thanks!"

Again he smiled at me. Just seeing him smile made me forget about my knee. I let go of my hair. It was barely long enough to blow in my face or knot and tangle. I lopped it off every summer to save on the heat against my neck. I also gave up not looking at him.

"You're not from around here are you?" I asked.

"Lily hasn't told you all about me already?"

I stifled a giggle and looked back toward the side of the road. I didn't dare repeat what she had told me.

"I was born in Gloucestershire, England where my father was the manager of hounds for the Duke of Beaufort's Hunt. My parents moved to Virginia when I was five and I grew up in Leesburg,

Virginia." When he started telling me where he was from, it got my attention and I looked back.

Edward kept his left hand at the ten o'clock position on the steering wheel and his right hand resting on the stick shift. I noticed far more about him than someone who wasn't supposed to get ideas should. Someone who wasn't completely enamored by him wouldn't have noticed how the hair on his arm that rested on the gear shift blew in the wind as it whirled through the truck from all directions or the little brown freckles sprinkled among the hair.

"What brought them to Virginia?" I inquired in an effort to keep up conversation and learn all I could about him.

"My father was offered a job as the manager of the hunt there."

"So you've been around horses and hounds all your life?"

"Yep. It's in my blood." Moving through the gears to change lanes in front of the old abandoned Dairy Queen, Edward asked, "What does your father do?"

I bit my lip and thought for a moment. No one had ever asked about my father's occupation before. Everyone I knew already knew about my father. The most direct and unfiltered answer was that my father pushed up daisies, but that was not an appropriate answer. Finally I came up with the words, again direct and to the point, but not crass.

"My father died when I was four."

There was a long moment of awkward silence. We went a half a mile before Edward spoke.

"Sorry about that. I didn't know."

"It's fine. It's odd, really, no one's ever asked me about him before. Thomson's such a small town that everyone I've ever met already knows what happened to him. You're the first person I've ever had to explain it all to."

This only seemed to pique Edward's curiosity. "We don't have to talk about it if you don't want to, but what happened to him?"

I held my face in my hands for a moment before spitting out the ugly truth. "He killed himself."

"What? Why? I've asked too much. We only just met. You don't have to tell me."

"No, it's alright, but we're almost there so you'll need to circle around for the whole story."

Instead of going straight on toward Hill Street, I had Edward make a right at the railroad tracks. As I explained to him about my father I forgot about giving him directions. We crossed over Hill Street by the hospital as I gave him the details I remembered of my father hanging himself. We wound up in Mr. Watson's driveway just as I recounted the sound the ceiling fan made and how I saw him there despite Mama's efforts to hide my eyes.

"I'm so sorry, Lucy." I liked it better when he called me Green.

It was such old news that I didn't remember anyone ever being sympathetic to me before. It wasn't just in his words, but it was written all over his face. Edward truly was sad for me and shocked at the turn our conversation had taken. He had such a chiseled face and every emotion he had was written across it.

"Please don't be. It happened so long ago."

"Still, it can't be easy to talk about." Edward shut off the truck and reached over and patted my hands which were now folded one on top of the other in my lap. He was so sweet.

By the time we made it to Mr. Watson's office, I was more infatuated with him. I could have talked with him for hours. We didn't have hours. We only had seconds. From her desk in the front window of the old house that was Mr. Watson's office, Mama saw us drive up and she came out. I introduced her to Edward. Mama was polite and thanked Edward for bringing me.

Mama was put out by my injury and having to use her lunch break to drive me to Nanny's house. The rest of the day felt like old times. I sat with my leg propped up on a pillow on top of the coffee table. That pillow was as good as cloud nine. Nanny and I shelled butter beans and watched one soap opera after another, but Edward was never far from my mind. Every conversation from my riding lesson played over and over in my head.

The rest of the week went by in virtual silence. Dwayne didn't say a word to me. He was clearly pissed off about my riding lesson and even more so that I didn't return to the kennel afterward, but I didn't care. What he failed to realize was that I was an only child and I liked quiet. If he thought I was going to be one of those girls that would beg him to talk to me, he had another thing coming. Not only did I like quiet, I had more than enough daydreams of Edward to occupy my time.

Friday afternoon's "quittin' time" was another joyous event. I was more than happy to be free of that place for the weekend. Unlike last Friday, I didn't get a, "Bye, Lucy, see you Monday." Instead there were no parting words from Dwayne, only the curling up of his right nostril, roll of his eyes and grunt as he threw open the door and left the kennel. So much for ladies first.

Knowing Mrs. Pope was behind me, I at least gave the appearance that I was taking the high road. 'Bye, Dwayne! Have a good weekend!" I called after him cheerfully as I caught the door he had just let fly.

Dwayne didn't say a word or throw up a hand. He just stormed on to slam the door to his old truck and revved the engine.

"I've seen some moody men in my time, but I think he takes the cake," Mrs. Pope added as she locked the door behind us.

I didn't say a word, I only gave her a knowing smile.

"Can I give you a ride?" Mrs. Pope offered.

"No, Ma'am. My mother should be here soon. Thank you anyway."

"All right then. If you need anything, Edward's over there at the apartment."

"Oh, okay. I'm sure I'll be fine. Mama should be here any moment."

Both Mama and I got off at 5:00 p.m. Mr. Watson's office was on the far side of town, across Hill Street, and in Friday afternoon traffic it would take Mama at least fifteen minutes to get to me.

As Mrs. Pope waved and drove away, I walked over to the old horse trailer that was basically yard art for the grounds at this point and took a seat on the bumper. As I sat there waiting, I prayed Edward would come out. He had sent word on Thursday through Mrs. Pope to inquire as to my knee, but I hadn't seen him since he dropped me off at Mr. Watson's office on Wednesday. It was hot out and sweat was sliding down my face and my spine. I wasn't at my best, but I would have given anything to have seen him.

I said a little prayer to God asking him to let me see Edward and much to my glorious surprise my prayer was almost immediately answered. It wasn't answered in quite the manner I had hoped, but nonetheless, I did see Edward. He walked right out of the end of the stable, got in his Bronco and drove away. I thanked God and then further clarified my request.

I swatted at some flies and added, "Dear Lord, I hate to be difficult, but next time could he see me too? Maybe say hello? Ask me out on a date? Well, yes, I guess that last one might be asking too much, but I did hear you are capable of miracles."

Before I got any more carried away with talking to myself and talking to the Lord, Mama showed up. I stood up as soon as I saw her. Instead of pulling up so that I could get in on the passenger side, she did the opposite. She shut the car off and opened her door.

"Do you want to practice?" She asked me. "Your test is going to be here before you know it."

I replied with delight, "Of course!" even though I didn't need any practice.

Nanny had been letting me drive since I was big enough to reach the pedals. I even drove us all the way to where the median wall starts on I-20 on the outskirts of Atlanta when I was twelve. Mama had no idea and if she found out she would have killed Nanny and me way back then.

On the ride home Mama and I made conversation about how our weeks went. The conversation was very limited since Mama took her job at the law office so seriously that she would rarely breathe a word about the place for fear of breaking some attorney-client code. The conversation was equally limited from my end as I dared not complain to her about the work at the kennel and I didn't want to give Dwayne the satisfaction of me telling my Mama on him.

When there was nothing else to talk about Mama finally asked, "How do you feel about missing the movies tonight? We've been invited to Boyd, I mean, Mr. Watson's house for dinner."

I didn't answer and pretended to focus on my driving. I slowed down and prepared to stop at the red light at the corner of Wally's convenience store.

Mama continued, "Lilly's cooking. She's been taking lessons from Molly and we are to be her guinea pigs tonight. It's just going to be us and the young man from the club."

"Young man from the hunt club?" I cut my eyes at her and tried to remain calm while screaming his name in question in my head.

"The one that's giving you lessons. I'm sorry, I can't remember his name."

I was so relieved that I forgot about driving. As I relaxed, I let my foot off the brake.

"Lucy!!!" Mama shrieked.

I slammed the brake and we narrowly missed rear-ending the car in front of us. Luckily the light changed and the guy in front gave it the gas.

Once Mama was able to speak again she confirmed that Edward would indeed be a guest of the Watson's that night. Without hesitation, I agreed to go to dinner, but covered my response. "I would love to see Lily."

I never cared much about what I wore before, but that evening it took me thirty minutes to decide which shirt and which pair of jean shorts to wear. Mama regularly made fun of me for always picking out the same clothes.

"Every shirt you own looks exactly the same," she always said.

I thought about all of that as I peeled one t-shirt after another out of my chest of drawers and tossed it on my bed. I couldn't help that I liked being comfortable, I told myself. Then, it occurred to me, maybe Mama was right. Maybe I should branch out. Maybe Edward would notice me if I dressed a little more like Whitney Knox. I looked up at the mirror on the dresser. Who was I kidding? There was no way I was leaving the house in a red tube top.

I picked a UGA t-shirt and some shorts and went on to stress about my hair. Dinner was at 6:30 and I only had time to wash my hair, but no time to straighten it. I almost always straightened it because if I didn't the humidity acted as a perming agent. I stared at myself in the mirror and pulled at the curls. It was no use. I pulled a bunch back from my face with a barrette and fretted some more.

"Lucy, come on!" Mama yelled.

I found my way to the living room where Mama was waiting. She was tapping a heel on the floor and a finger on her watch. "We're going to be late."

Mama was dressed to the nine's and I looked like I did every other Friday night.

"It's not like he's going to make you punch the clock is he?" I rolled my eyes.

"Lucy." With one word, my name, I knew Mama was not amused. She never was when I made smart remarks concerning Mr. Watson.

Mama let go of the chastising look she was giving me and went to get her purse on the way toward the door leading from the kitchen to the carport.

"Can I drive?" I asked as I followed her.

"No."

"But you said I need to practice."

"I also told you to be more grateful toward Mr. Watson, but we see how that's going."

I rolled my lips in a huff much like the horses at the club did when the flies were getting the better of them.

Chapter 4

Mama zig-zagged around behind the shopping center with the Piggly Wiggly, past the Dozier's house, over the railroad tracks and made a left on to Lee Street. The Watson's lived around the hard curve on Lee Street.

A lot of the old money people of Thomson lived on Lee Street and most of the new money people lived at Three Chimneys, the private country club on the north side of town. It used to be the even richer side of the Watson family's home place, but all that was left after the house burned to the ground like fat lighter was the three stacked stone chimneys and two thousand acres.

Some folks with no money dreamed of living in a new house at the country club and others had dreams like mine. I dreamed of living on Lee Street.

It was on the opposite side of the street from the McNeil house and that was a Thomson landmark. The Watson house was white with columns, a wrap-around porch and was bigger than any other house I had ever been inside. It was the classic Greek revival style. Its neighbor might have been a landmark, but this was a real jewel of the South.

The windows on the front of the house were each as big as the door on our house and the shutters were real working shutters. If a storm came, they could still pull them closed if they wanted. By the front door of the Watson house, the lamps still operated off of gas. They were little flickering flames which reminded me of the one I'd seen on TV that lit President Kennedy's grave, the eternal flame they called it. Everything about the Watson house was grand.

It was built during the reconstruction period between the end of the Civil War and the turn of the century. It had been in their family for three generations. Mr. Watson had lived there all his life, but it had only just become his about three years ago when his mother died. One day it would be Lily's.

It was funny. As Mama and I walked up the sidewalk to the front door I noticed the handprints in the cement in front of the bottom step. In 1985 Mr. Watson had the old walkway busted up and a new one laid. I happened to be there that day and when Mr. Watson pressed Lily's hands into the wet mush, she insisted mine go in right next to hers. He would do anything for her so my tiny little hands are right next to hers. With her index finger, Lily wrote, "Lily and Lucy, sisters forever," under the indentions. Lily envied me and being able to have a job, but I had always envied her of her house. When we were little, I wished we were sisters so I could live there too.

It was a short walk up the pavement from where Mama parked in the driveway. While I was taking in my surroundings and how they hadn't changed much in all the years I had been coming there, my stomach was starting to knot with nervousness. Edward's truck wasn't there yet. What if he didn't come and I had agreed to dine with Boyd Watson for nothing? As I took the first step on the porch, I glanced back at the handprints once more and tried to remember that there had been good times with Mr. Watson. Maybe if Edward didn't come, I would focus on remembering the good times and that would get me through.

"Do you want to ring the doorbell?" Mama pulled my attention back to the present.

"I'm not five," I snapped back and as soon as I did I regretted it.

"So pushing buttons on elevators is no longer your thing either?" Every now and then Mama could hold her own with the witty comebacks, but those times were rare.

I liked to think I wasn't a typical teenage girl, but this time I behaved like one, disappointed about a boy and moody toward authority. I rolled my eyes and turned up my nose.

"Don't worry. I'll get it." Mama reached forward and pressed the doorbell.

To her credit, there was a time when I would have mowed her over to press the button for the doorbell at the Watson's. The bell played the same tune as the horn from the General Lee, the car on "The Dukes of Hazard." It was so loud one could definitely hear it out on the porch and one could probably hear it all the way to Hall Street. I used to find it amusing, but now it was annoying.

My back was turned, but when the door opened I could hear how desperate it was for WD-40. The sound was a high pitched, "Eeek," sound that made the hair on the back of my neck stand up. The hair stood up even more when I heard his voice.

"Come on in y'all." He opened the door wider and Mama headed inside. "Lily's in the kitchen. She's almost done."

I didn't follow. I lingered there on the porch, looking down the street. Where was Edward?

Mama wore heels everywhere. The clacking of them stopped on the hardwood floor of the foyer. "Lucy, are you coming?"

"Yes, ma'am." I turned around to find Mr. Watson still holding the door for me and Mama waiting just inside. She shook her head in disappointment while I tried to hide the same sentiment on my face. I was disappointed that Edward wasn't there yet.

I was barely inside when Lily came running, well, running as best she could. "Lucy!" She wiped her hands on her apron just before she threw her arms around me. "I'm so glad you could make it!" She beamed.

With the smell of fried chicken filling my nostrils and Lily hugging me, I was momentarily distracted and allowed myself a moment of happiness. "Thanks for inviting me."

Lily pulled back from me and just smiled an infectious smile.

Under her apron, Lily had on a long flowing cotton dress. It was sky blue with stems of daisies growing from the hem up the dress. It looked like she was constantly walking in a field of flowers.

Mama had on a wrap dress and all of us had on more make-up than would be fit for daylight. Everyone had dressed for dinner except Mr. Watson. He was still in a pair of khaki shorts and a white shirt with the Three Chimneys golf course's logo on it. He looked like he had strolled in from the course, taken a nap and only woke to the sound of the doorbell. He hadn't even bothered to put on shoes.

Mr. Watson showed Mama to the living room while Lily and I discussed her accomplishments in the kitchen.

"Do you need any help?" I asked her. "I can set a pretty mean table."

"That would be great! Daddy was supposed to do that, but he can't tear himself away from the T.V. The Braves are playing." Lily took a sideways glance in the direction of the living room before starting down the hall toward the back of the house.

The living room was the first door on the right of the foyer. The foyer was essentially a long hallway that contained a series of doors and the staircase and split the house in half, straight down the middle. Standing in the front door, one could see right out the back door.

The interior of the house hadn't changed a bit since the last time I was there. Every picture on the wall, every squeak in the floor, everything was exactly the same. Everywhere I looked there was a memory of some afternoon I spent playing in this house with Lily.

The kitchen was on the opposite side of the house of the living and dining rooms. I followed Lily to the kitchen passing by the staircase and remembering the most vivid memory I had of playing with Lily. The memory was of Molly spanking me one afternoon. Lily dared me to see how many steps I could jump. Molly told us to stop, but as soon as she went back to watching As the World Turns, I jumped again and with a hard thud, I crashed into the back of the front door. Before I could shake it off, Molly had me by the wrist and was wearing my little behind out. She was the only person other than my mother that had ever spanked me.

I was cross with Molly for spanking me and I told Mama as soon as she picked me up that afternoon. Mama said I got what I deserved and told Molly, "It takes a village."

The shock of it made an impression and that was the last time I ever disobeyed Molly. It was also the last time I ever jumped down a staircase.

Once in the kitchen Lily checked on the chicken still frying on the stove. "You remember where the china is."

"How could I forget?"

Of course china was kept in the china cabinet and china cabinets were in dining rooms, but remembering where a china cabinet was not the jest of the memory.

"You really loved to try Molly's patience," Lily laughed.

"Well, tea parties called for china even if the guests were stuffed." I folded my arms and acted as if I didn't see a problem at all.

"Luckily Molly heard you drag over the chair and got to you before you could pull out any of my mother's china and drop it. You were always a clumsy little thing."

"And you think I'm not now? You think I'm safe to touch your mother's china now?"

I took down the china and as I set the table, I remembered the time Lily and I hauled out every quilt and blanket in the house and built a fort under the dining room table. I had so many memories of playing with Lily here when I was little, but this was one of my favorites. We draped the quilts and blankets over the table and across the backs of the chairs and made a tunnel between the legs of the chairs. I could still see it, a redneck circus tent of patchwork quilts and electric blankets. I straightened the forks around the plates and laughed at the thought.

"What's so funny, Green?" A deep voice came from the doorway. I didn't even have to look up to know who it was. It was Edward. Who else called me 'Green'?

My stomach did flips and I felt the fever in my cheeks. I bit my bottom lip to keep from grinning from ear to ear. "It's nothing."

"That little laugh wasn't over nothing." He waited. "Tell me."

I moved on to the next place setting and put down the knife and spoon to the right of the plate. "We used to build forts and tunnels using this table and chairs when we were children."

I raised my eyes from my task just barely. Edward was so attractive that it almost hurt to look at him.

"I sometimes miss those days," I added. "I know it's silly."

"Edward, is that you?" Lily called from the kitchen.

"I guess I should offer to help her," Edward nodded toward the direction of her voice.

"I'm sure she would appreciate that." I moved on to the next plate after finishing with the dinner and salad forks.

Edward stepped toward the doorway that led back into the hall, but stopped and looked back. "It's not silly. There's hardly a day that goes by that I don't miss playing with my sisters."

When Lily was finally done, she invited us to the table and assigned each of us a seat. Naturally, Mr. Watson was seated at the head of the table. Lily sat to his right and Mama to his left. Lily sat Edward next to her and me next to Mama. That also meant I was across from Edward.

Dinner was enlightening. I hadn't noticed when we first arrived, but Lily had on more make-up than I'd ever seen her wear. I suppose one could say the same about me, but I had a mother to send me back to the bathroom to wipe some of mine off. Lily didn't have that and she looked like a character off of a Technicolor movie, just too much.

Lily prodded Edward to tell us what he had been up to lately and how things were going at the hunt club. He was clearly uncomfortable talking about the club in front of Mr. Watson.

"I'm sure not everyone is as trying as Lucy when it comes to giving riding lessons," Mama commented and I nudged her under the table.

I could have died. I kept my head down and paid more attention to cutting my chicken than the average person would.

Mr. Watson picked up his chicken and bit into it. He could be counted on to make whatever situation I had a little more unbearable and this time he did it while chomping on a drumstick. "I'm sure she'll get the hang of it by the end of summer."

By the end of summer? Nevertheless embarrassed, I saw that as a challenge.

"She's not that bad." Edward took a swig of tea and then sat down his glass. "I think she'll have the hang of it in another lesson or two."

Although I wasn't looking at him spot on, Edward appeared to be forming the beginning of his next sentence when Lily cut him off.

"Edward, how did your sister enjoy her visit last week?" Lily changed the subject and I got the distinct feeling that I had received my fair share of attention for the night.

"She had a fine time."

"That was nice of her to come all the way down from Virginia to see you." Lily batted her overly caked eyelashes.

I'm sure there was a curious look on my face. I was beginning to get the picture, but I didn't say a word.

"Would you like another helping of mashed potatoes?" Lily offered him.

"No thanks."

"I'll take another helping." Mr. Watson held out his hand for Lily to pass the plate, but she didn't even acknowledge him. I almost laughed out loud. The thought that someone would dare ignore him was priceless to me since every time he said "Jump," my mother asked "How high?"

Edward proceeded to correct Lily about his sister. "Oh, my sister didn't come all the way just to see me. They were on their way to take my niece to Disney World and stopped by long enough for me to go with them to the place where they make the Cabbage Patch Kid Dolls in Cleveland."

"You went to Babyland General?" Mama asked. "Lucy used to love going there."

It was like everyone had to continually remind Edward that I was a child.

"How many Cabbage Patch Kids do you have, Lucy?" Edward asked me and I nearly choked on my green beans.

I was two coughs into trying to get her string beans out of my windpipe when Lily piped up. "I had four."

I had never hated Lily before but I hated her for a moment as I got my throat clear. I noticed Mr. Watson nudge her hand. When she looked at him to see what he wanted he gave her a sideways jiggle of his head suggesting she need not say anything else on the subject.

The truth was we were too poor for me to have more than one doll and it certainly didn't come from Babyland General. It came from Santa which I now knew was code for Daddy and the clearance rack at Service Merchandise.

Mama didn't take the hint that Mr. Watson gave Lily. "She had one. In fact, she still has it. Don't you Lucy?"

"Yes, ma'am," I said with a sharp tone.

"For the life of me I can't figure out why she won't get rid of that thing," she went on.

Maybe if I put more food on her plate she would eat and stop talking. "Mama, would you like another piece of chicken?" I knew better than to ask, but I had to try something. Mama was one of those Southern ladies that didn't like to eat in public, but we were about to go down a road I knew she didn't really want to go down.

"No, Lucy, you know..." She stopped herself and I sat the plate of chicken down. "I'm throwing out that doll when we get home."

The thought infuriated me and stung my heart at the same time. "You'll do no such thing!"

Mama's head twitched in pure shock at how I had just spoken to her. She looked around behind her as one does when they suspect they are not the intended recipient of the statement. Of course there was no one behind her. She put her fork and knife down. "Excuse me? What did you just say?"

"Mary, would you like some pie?" Mr. Watson again tried to steer the conversation, but failed.

"No, Boyd." She emphasized his name. "I would not care for any pie! I would like for Lucy to explain herself."

"Are you sure about that?" I didn't back down.

Again, her head twitched a little and all the curls on her head jiggled. This time her jaw dropped as well.

69

"Lily, get the God-damn pie!" Mr. Watson ordered. "Mary, give it a rest. Lucy, apologize to your mother."

I hadn't ever heard Mr. Watson speak to any of us like that before, let alone Lily.

As I threw down my head in defiance, Lily excused herself to the kitchen to get the Lemon Icebox Pie that she had made for dessert.

"NO!" I straightened my shoulders and puffed out my chest.

It no longer mattered that Edward was there. Anything that related to Daddy was off limits for me as far as Mama was concerned so I figured the same went for her. He gave me that doll. It and a few pictures were all I had left of him. She was not about to throw it away. I would go to my grave before I let her take it.

"You will apologize to your mother young lady!" His eyes looked bloodshot with rage. I had never seen him mad before, but he had never seen me mad either and I had plenty to be mad about.

"No! And who are you to make me?"

It was on the tip of my tongue, but I held back. If Mama had taught me anything, it was holding back. Holding back from ever telling exactly how I felt was always in my best interest. Telling how I felt about something, giving my opinion, would only make things worse. She only wanted a smiling face with no words and no thoughts of my own. I was in enough trouble, spitting fire at her hero, Mr.

Watson. Shouting at the dinner table that he was not my father would only make things worse.

Mr. Watson's face turned red and he stood up from the table. His chair went sliding across the dining room behind him. He didn't even excuse himself as he left the room.

"Lucy Ann Meeks, I will deal with you later!" Mama huffed as she whipped her napkin from her lap and violently hurled it onto the table. She flew up out of her seat and chased after Mr. Watson. With the force that Mama threw that cloth napkin, it might have gone clear through the plate, the table and the floor beneath if it had been her fork instead. She clearly wanted to put that napkin under the house.

Lily was out of the room at that point and probably missed the last of the battle. Edward witnessed the entire thing, but he was an afterthought.

I had never disagreed with Mama in public before and I had rarely done it in private. Sometimes she was a reasonable woman, but this was not one of those times. If she had just thought about the doll before trying to impress everyone with her iron fisted style of parenting, she might have remembered its significance to me.

Mama didn't do that. She didn't think of me at all and she didn't think of my father either. As far as I knew she never thought of him, but I thought of him all the time. I wondered if he were still around, would she treat me like I was just an accessory to her life as she did now. I wondered if she would have been kinder had he not left us the way he did. Mama did exactly what I knew she would do. She thought of Mr. Watson first, not me. I wondered what my father would think of that.

The argument had happened so fast, but now I was left in silence. I pushed my plate back and looked up at Edward. He was the only one left at the table with me.

"Sorry I ruined dinner."

He snickered. "You didn't ruin anything. This was the most entertaining meal I've had over here."

"You eat here often?" I asked as I started to fiddle with my napkin and fold it into different shapes, a fan, and then a triangle.

"About twice a week."

"Really?" I continued to fold the napkin.

"Yes. Lily and I are friends."

"Ah," I remembered her make-up and the strange way she was trying to manipulate the conversation. "Friends."

"So tell me, what's the big deal with the doll?" Edward was the only one with good sense to ask me.

"My dad gave it to me before he died. I'll probably have to see a shrink one day since I associate my doll with my father."

"So you feel like the doll connects you to him?"

"It does. He handed it to me right before..." I paused. I'd smothered the spirit of dinner enough without getting into how my dad killed himself, plus Edward and I had touched on that when he gave me a ride the other day. "Anyway, it's like having a piece of him."

"Oh, Lucy, I'm so sorry." I hadn't realized, but Mama was standing in the doorway and so was Lily. Mama had heard everything, but I'm not sure how much Lily had heard.

My mother had never apologized to me before, but she apologized to me then and I had witnesses. I'm not sure whether I was more stunned or embarrassed now by the whole debacle.

Mama had tears in her eyes and again I lost sight of Edward. "I didn't know."

"If you all don't mind, I'm just going to go. It's been..." Edward struggled for the proper word to describe the experience that had been dinner at the Watson's. As he stood from his chair he added the word "interesting."

Edward said his good-byes. He shook hands with Mama and hugged Lily. She appeared to melt in his arms.

Edward hugged me too and whispered, "Chin up, Green. Things will work out."

The proximity to him was almost unbearable. My head swirled, but I managed to squeak out the word, "Thanks."

While Mama fretted over me and having hurt my feelings, Lily all but chased Edward to his truck, begging him to stay. She returned empty handed to find Mama and myself gathering ourselves to leave as well.

"Awe, y'all aren't leaving too?" Lily was visibly disappointed.

"I'm sorry we ruined your dinner." Mama said as she gently hugged her.

"Me too. The food was wonderful." What I ate of it.

"I guess we'll have to do it again sometime. Y'all were good sports about being my guinea pigs."

Mama excused herself to say goodnight to Mr. Watson who had gone back to the solitude of the living room and the remaining innings of the Braves game.

"Go on to the car Lucy, I'll be right there."

I did like she asked. I finished my good-bye with Lily, begged her forgiveness for how the night had gone and headed toward the front door. The windows of the house were old. I don't know how old, but they weren't the double-paned ones that saved energy like the ones in our house. They were the old single-paned style that were barely held together by crackling ridges. I only noticed the windows because they didn't contain the screaming coming from Mr. Watson and Mama that bled right through them.

"We can't keep hiding the truth!" Mr. Watson screamed.

"Lower your voice!" Mama went back at him.

"You know I'm right. She's going to figure it out and when she does we'll all be sorry."

"She's my daughter and…"

Lily came out on to the porch carrying two plates loaded with left-overs and wrapped in tinfoil. I couldn't hear the rest of what Mama was saying.

Foiled again, I thought as Lily handed me the plates. I really wanted to hear what they were fighting about.

"We'll never eat all of this," Lily explained. "I wish I had thought to make Edward a plate."

Seems I wasn't the only one with Edward constantly on the brain. Lily waited with me until Mama came out. I couldn't hear anything further coming through the windows and that disappointed me. I was curious to know why Mama and Mr. Watson would be fighting and what truth was it that I needed to be told. I had a suspicion about what it was, but I didn't know for sure. I had wondered for a long time if they were having an affair. The way she talked about him, hung on his every thought and action, what else was I supposed to think?

I didn't like it, but it beat the bejeebers out of the alternative. At least it wasn't about poor dear Lily again. The last secret they held to themselves was that Lily's cancer had returned. I figured after the fit I threw last time, they'd tell me if that's what it was. Surely, they would tell me. Lily would tell me.

Chapter 5

"I thought I was being helpful. The horse trailer was rocking like it was going to tip over." Describing myself as embarrassed was an understatement. It had been a rough few weeks and this was just the cherry on top.

"Why did you open the door to the trailer?" Mrs. Pope was a practical woman. She was stern like someone who devoted their lives to training dogs would have to be.

"I don't know. So I could tell what was going on when I went for help. I thought the horse in there was going to hurt itself." I held my face in my hands and covered my mouth, still in shock of what I had witnessed.

"No one in there was being hurt. At least no more than they were asking for it."

I blushed, but Mrs. Pope acted as if this was a common occurrence around the hunt club.

She wiped the sweat from her brow and tried to smooth down her wiry gray hair.

"Well, you learned a valuable lesson."

Bewilderment replaced the embarrassment on my face.

Mrs. Pope continued, "You learned if the horse trailer's rockin' don't go knockin' and for heaven's sake don't look inside!"

She had a nice belly laugh after she finished her statement. I suppose she had a point, but I didn't find it funny. If I had only noticed the horse tied to the other side of the trailer that might have stopped me, but maybe not. I had a compulsion to try to be helpful and that sometimes got me into trouble. This time I was definitely in trouble. My eyes could never un-see Mr. Channel, one of the oldest members of the hunt in nothing, but his riding boots while he was being ridden by Whitney Knox. Even worse was that they saw me too. He looked purely panic stricken, just like me, but she didn't break her stride. She gave him two smacks with the riding crop as I slammed the door shut and bolted back to the barn.

Mrs. Pope was the first person I ran into when I returned. She immediately suspected something was wrong. I was drained of all color and she noticed.

"Have you seen a ghost, child?"

"No, ma'am."

I could have left it at that, but she was concerned and wouldn't let me go until I told her what the matter was. After talking with her, I only felt slightly better.

This was my first time ever catching anyone in the act. I didn't have a mother and a father or a mother and a step-father like my friends. I'd never busted in on anyone before, let alone folks that were brazenly having an affair.

Talk about how the other half lived, my grandfather would have died before he got caught with his fly down in public let alone with his britches altogether off and flung ten feet away in some hay. Furthermore, any of my friends would have cringed to the point of convulsions at the thought of doing *that* with one of their grandfather's friends. Not to mention, the horse trailer, I had an imagination and I was no stranger to soap operas or lust, but never in my wildest thoughts would a horse trailer been a suitable accommodation for me.

All of these thoughts ran through my head as I returned to my seat next to Lily. It was my first night being invited to dinner at the hunt. Both Mr. Watson and Lily insisted that I stay and they were my ride home so I didn't have much of a choice. I was stuck there until they decided to leave.

Every Wednesday night after the hunt, one of the members hosted dinner. Tonight the Harpers hosted and they provided the main dish, a Low Country Boil. Other members added side dishes and dessert.

During dinner things went fine. While we ate, Lily and I had listened as Edward, Mr. Harper, The Master of the Hounds and the other whips rehashed how they chased down a red fox. They interrupted one another, each vying for the attention of Mr. Watson and giving their version of events. This appeared to be the first time in quite a while that he had not been in the thick of things with them.

"Did you see the fox?" Lily asked me.

I hurried and chewed the bite of corn on the cob I had just taken. "No. I was so far in the back of the field that binoculars wouldn't have even helped."

"Maybe next time."

"I don't know. I don't think I'd like to see the little animal get..."

Lily knew what I was getting at. "They try to stop the hounds before that happens."

Lily was so naïve and I guess I had been too. The hounds were trained to hunt. What did she expect they were going to do? I understood that all along, but that didn't mean I wanted to see it or that I liked the idea of killing the fox for sport. I could have gone on telling Lily about my moral misgivings as to the fox hunt, but instead I chose to keep the rest of my opinions to myself. That's when I told Lily I was going to change my shoes.

After dinner, when I got back, she noticed that I hadn't changed out of my riding boots at all. "I thought you were going to the car to change shoes."

I didn't want to be the town gossip so I told her, "I figure I'll never get these things broken in if I don't wear them."

My answer was reasonable and the color had returned to my face so there was no need for Lily to pry further.

"You look cute in your riding attire," Lily nudged me.

"Thanks. So do you." I winked back.

Mr. Watson had sent an entire riding outfit home with Mama for me on Monday. Lily said her dad felt bad about the way things had gone on Friday night so they spent their entire Sunday afternoon at the tack store in Augusta buying proper riding clothes for me. Lily also scored an outfit. It was his way of apologizing to her for ruining her first dinner party as well.

My mother had done her own apologizing all weekend long. Mama's apologies didn't come in the form of gifts. They came in the form of answers.

The ride home on Saturday night was silent. Mama let me drive again and, all the way home, I worked up the courage to ask about Mr. Watson.

Our phone was ringing off the hook when we walked in. It was Maggie calling from 4-H camp, but I told her I couldn't talk. By the time I got off of the phone with Maggie, Mama had changed into her pajamas. In the time it took me to change into my own pajamas, Mama popped microwave popcorn. I joined her on the couch and started watching a rerun of JAG.

The television in the living room was the only color TV in the house and the only one that had cable. I found myself looking at the TV more than the show playing on it. The TV was yet another example of Mr. Watson's presence in our home.

"Why are so many things in our house gifts from Mr. Watson?"

Mama hadn't seen that one coming and just about snorted the popcorn through her nose. She lost one of her house slippers in her flailing about to breathe and coughing up the popcorn. She doubled over and hacked while I recited a list of the things in our house that Mr. Watson gave us.

"The TV, the microwave, the wingback chair over there, my bedroom suite..." Getting a hold of herself Mama replied, "Your bedroom suite was a hand-me-down from Lily. He had nothing to do with that. Lily wanted you to have it."

I remembered my prior headboard and dresser and there was nothing wrong with them. "What I had was fine and I'm serious. You work for him, but he's constantly in our lives. It's like you never get off work and everywhere we look in this house, there he is." I pointed at the TV and the leather hobnail chair that was the nicest thing in the room.

"Why all the questions?" Mama deflected again.

"I just wondered why. It's not normal."

Mama was getting that look, the one she gets when she's nervous. Her eyes got bigger and she started to randomly scratch at spots on her arms and neck. It was as if she had some sort of rash.

"Really, Lucy? There's nothing sinister about Boyd Watson. He's my boss and he's just a nice guy."

I grunted. Why couldn't she just be honest with me? There was something strange going on with them, I just knew it.

Mama didn't like the grunt. Her guilt was wearing off. "Exactly what do you think is going on then?"

Now there was a question I wasn't about to answer. If I'd told her I thought they were having an affair she'd slap my face.

I gave a defeated sigh, "Never mind," and I ended the conversation.

Sitting next to Lily and thinking about everything that had gone on lately, I decided I would ask her. Just as when I asked Mama, it took me a few minutes to decide how to phrase the question, but finally I came out with it.

"Lily, why does your dad buy us so much stuff and give us all of y'all's hand-me-downs?"

Lily had been listening to the elder club men tell stories about the hunt when I interrupted. No one else could hear me and it took Lily a second to answer.

"I don't know," Lily shrugged.

"Do you think they're having an..." My heart fluttered at the sight of Edward and I lost my train of thought.

"Hello, ladies, Lily, Green."

I had watched him discretely all through dinner. I couldn't help it. He moved through all of the members of the hunt like a knife through butter. All of the ladies ogled over him and he made the men miss their youth. Even smeared in a bit of blood from the fox the hounds killed and dripping with his own sweat from the summer heat and the uniform jacket of the hunt, he was still gorgeous. From nine to ninety, they either wanted him or wanted to be him. There wasn't a member there who hadn't stood in line to engage Edward in conversation.

Edward wasted no time getting to business. He hadn't stopped by just to chat. "If you're done with dinner would you mind helping me? We've got a couple of hounds that haven't made it back and with Dwayne gone..."

"But we're supposed to give her a ride home," Lily objected. "You could be out for hours trying to round them up."

I didn't have a chance to say yes or no before Edward assured her that he would see that I got home.

"I'll come to help too."

Edward looked Lily over. He was too polite to be blunt and tell her why she couldn't come. She wasn't fit enough to hold a lap dog let alone chase down one of the wildlings as I might have to do. He chose his words well before he countered her offer.

"It's her job. It wasn't really a question and I can't justify paying both of you. Come on, Green. As Lily pointed out, this may take hours so we should get started."

I could see the turning of wheels in her head when he called me Green again. Lily was trying to figure out what that was about.

Edward started toward the door and I stood up. I was going to turn back to tell her goodnight and not to worry about me, but Lily grabbed my wrist.

"Why does he call you that?"

"I don't know."

Lily studied my face and then released me. I didn't see the harm in Lily riding along with us and I felt bad having to leave her. But I didn't mind spending time alone with Edward either. Despite Edward describing our mission as work for me, Lily looked defeated and skeptical of my answer about him calling me Green. I was sure she felt left out. The truth of the matter was that she didn't have many friends, if any. The time this summer with me and Edward was the most interaction I had ever seen her have with anyone outside of her immediate family.

"I'll call you and let you know I got home okay." I patted Lily on the shoulder.

Lily mustered a flat smile in return.

As Edward instructed, I ran to the kennel and grabbed the tracker while he pulled the Bronco around.

Edward circled in front of the kennel and slowed down enough to reach across and throw open the passenger side door. I was barely out of the kennel door when he yelled, "Grab some flashlights! We're losing daylight."

I returned with the tracker and the only flashlight I could find and hopped in the truck. I was hardly in, let alone buckled up, but Edward gave it the gas and I slid sideways in my seat. I squealed and grabbed the dash hard enough to leave indentions from my nails.

Edward threw back his head and laughed. It wasn't the first time he had been wild that day. The tires spun and kicked up dust all over the cars, trucks and horse trailers parked in front of the kennel, but I reflected on my lesson from earlier in the day.

"Mr. Watson wants you ready to take the field with the hunt today so you're getting a crash course."

We'd skipped the lesson yesterday so it seemed natural that we would pick-up with it another day. I didn't think it would be today since they told me to begin with that they didn't want my lessons on the same day they took the field. I guess that didn't matter after all.

Edward was on a quarter-horse in front of me and when he sucked his teeth, he gave the horse a jolt in the sides with his heels. His horse accelerated to a run.

I was on Blueberry and quickly learned that horses were herding animals. Blueberry picked up speed and I held on for dear life, but after a few of seconds, I wasn't terrified anymore.

Edward leaned forward in the saddle and I found that to be a natural position as well. I was squatted in the stirrups, with a hunched back and

85

hands wrapped around the reins. Unlike posting, Blueberry did all the work and I just held on. This was fun.

I watched Edward and before I knew it, I was fearless. Blueberry and I started out chasing him. Then, we weren't chasing any longer. We were keeping up. Several times he looked back, checking on me with a look of concern. As I caught up with him the look on his face changed. Wide-eyed, he was stunned that I was keeping up and actually gaining on me. We were in the wide open pasture so it wasn't like I was going to get lost. From one end to the other, it stretched a quarter mile so he could see me. The last time he looked back, Blueberry's nose was even with his saddle. The look on his face changed to that of a competitor, not a teacher. His jaw tightened as if to signal his determination. I wasn't one to back off from a little competition. I did everything he was doing and I urged Blueberry on. I beat Edward to the far side of the pasture and back twice.

Edward wasn't the only one that had been wild. I wanted him to show me how to jump, but he refused.

"We've got to save something for next time." I was fine with that answer because that meant there would be a next time.

During the hunt Edward rode with the other whips. Mr. Watson was a whip too, but this time he stayed behind in the field with me. The field was what they called the rest of us who weren't going full force chasing the hounds.

The whips kept up with the hounds. It wasn't called a hunt for nothing. The hounds really did hunt and today they picked up the scent of a fox.

Mr. Watson had a walkie-talkie and we could hear them through it and we could hear the barking of the hounds in the distance. Aside from the fact that I didn't get to see very much, riding with Mr. Watson wasn't nearly as fun as riding with Edward.

We turned out and headed away from town. Edward drove with one hand and fiddled with the tracker with the other. The tracker was a glorified walkie-talkie like device with what looked like a weather map on it. I was glad he knew what he was doing because I didn't have a clue. It was yet another thing Dwayne was supposed to show me how to work, but couldn't seem to find the time.

For the first time I watched Edward and didn't care if he noticed me. I didn't know him that well and I really didn't know Dwayne that well, but what I did know is that he was a much better man than Dwayne. It wasn't about looks. It was about how Edward expected the best from me and made me rise to the occasion. Dwayne seemed hell-bent on keeping me in my place and that place seemed to be wherever he decided.

Edward held up the tracking device. "See each dog has a collar and the collar is programmed in here. See the light blinking? That's our pup."

I leaned over toward him as he held it out to me. That was the first time I'd heard anyone in the club refer to one of the hounds as anything akin to what one would call pet.

Edward's foot was heavy on the gas pedal and he was paying more attention to the red blip on the tracking device than the road as we flew along. The sun was just starting to set and this was the coolest night of the summer so far. With the top down and the wind whipping through my hair, my arms had chill bumps. I wished I had my riding jacket which I'd left in Mr. Watson's truck before dinner.

As I rubbed my arms and folded them together for warmth, I wondered if Edward even owned a top to this thing.

The fact that I was freezing was just as concerning as Edward's driving, but when he barely slowed up to make the turn down an old field road, his driving became the bigger concern.

"Whoa!" I screamed. Despite the seatbelt I bounced clean out of my seat. "Slow down! Jesus!"

Edward took his eyes off the tracker and the tire track road long enough to look at me and chuckle.

"It's not funny!" I scolded him. "If this thing had a ceiling, you would have cracked my skull on it!"

We crossed the field in a matter of seconds, each one pounded out by the tires on the rivets made by a plow in the dry dirt. The far side of the field had an opening in the woods where the tire tracks continued.

It was a logging road that had been long since abandoned. Again it was made of two tire tracks, but they were well on their way to being lost to nature as the space between them. The over growth of saplings and wild bush that had taken over the middle of the road didn't slow Edward down. There was a definite sense that time was of the essence and I didn't think that was just because of it getting dark out.

When Edward did slow down we were quite possibly a mile and a half back in the woods and about four miles from the kennel. His foot was as hard on the brake as it was on the gas and we came to a sliding halt. The back end of the Bronco fishtailed and I grabbed for the dash to steady myself once more especially when we swiped a pine that was way more than just a sapling.

"That's going to leave a dent." I cut my eyes to the point of impact.

"Shhh! Be quiet!"

The look on Edward's face was sheer determination. The tracker was still in his hand, but he wasn't looking at it anymore. He was just listening and I listened with him.

"Did you hear that?" His head darted to the right and he looked past me, his eyes wide as he focused on the thick forest.

Beyond the crickets and singing tree frogs I didn't hear anything unusual, but I tried.

"From over there!" Edward leaned against me and pointed in the direction of a large Dogwood tree.

I felt flushed at his proximity to me, but I also knew that if anything, even the missing hound, jumped out of those trees right then, I would pee my pants.

I heard a low whimper and I caught my breath. If that was the hound, it was hurt.

"Let's go." Edward threw down the tracker and jumped out of the Bronco. I was hardly unbuckled when I looked back to find him holding out his hand to me, offering to help me out. The thing might not have had a door for him to open for me, but he was still a gentleman.

Like every other crop of trees around, the pines were harvested, replanted and left to fend for themselves for twenty or so years until it was time to cut them again. These pines had been long since abandoned and were likely approaching their prime. The underbrush was thick and over grown with wiry vines, thorny ones and poison ivy all over the place.

Edward started through the thickness and held back each branch for me to pass behind him without one flying back and smacking me. He acted as if it was my first walk in a forest, but it wasn't. Nanny and I often walked far into the woods behind her house to pick blackberries. I knew to watch for flying branches as well as where I put my feet as not to step on a snake. I knew to walk about five feet behind so the branches wouldn't fly back and hit me, but every time I fell back, he stopped and waited on me.

The whimpering and whining of the hound got louder the farther into the trees we went. We found the animal about thirty yards from the Bronco. The poor thing was a pitiful sight. It had gotten its right hind leg wrapped in what was left of a barbed wire fence. The more the sad animal had twisted to get free the more entangled it became. The white fur of its back end was dripping red with blood.

I covered my mouth and gasped. I was squeamish over my own blood, but normally fine seeing someone else's. This was different. I froze where I stood for fear of being revisited by the shrimp and corn I had just eaten.

While I stood in fear, Edward dropped to his knees for a closer look. I watched as he laid a hand on the dog's head. Its eyes rolled back and it stopped crying for a moment. Edward stroked his muzzle and comforted the poor thing. The dog fell still and Edward whispered to it.

"It's gonna be okay."

His voice was soothing and seemed to be having the same effect on me as it was the dog. My stomach was settling and I was adjusting to the circumstances. Seeing the animal, pitiful as it was, my heart broke for it.

Edward lowered his face to the shoulder of his white shirt and wiped a tear away with his sleeve.

"Lucy," he didn't call me "Green" then and I noticed the catch in his throat when he said my name. "Go get what's in the glove box and bring it to me."

Halfway back to the tuck and it occurred to me what Mama kept in her glove box. I don't know what I thought when he first gave me the instruction, wire cutters maybe to cut the hound free. No one in their right mind kept wire cutters in their glove compartment, but I had seen stranger that night. Who in their right mind got it on in a horse trailer?

I slapped my forehead and kept walking. Sure enough, I found a 380 in the glove box. I cringed at what was going to happen and my eyes started to sting as I fought off the tears.

Half of my life was spent growing up in the house on Dixie Drive in Thomson and the other half on Nanny and Papa's farm on the outskirts of town. They used to have goats and various other barnyard animals. Although it was unpleasant, Papa occasionally had to put one out of its misery. Of course it wasn't a decision Papa took lightly. There was nothing else that he could do; the animal had to be put down.

I took the gun out and lingered by the truck for a moment. Just because I knew it was a necessary evil, didn't make it any easier. I could hardly put one foot in front of the other to go back. I knew I must. I couldn't let the poor thing suffer. I wiped my eyes and headed back.

A machete would have made the trek a little quicker, but I dared not run with what was clearly a loaded gun in my hand. I'd never held one before. I'd never had to do the job myself. I didn't envy Edward having to do it either. I couldn't imagine.

With each step I could hear the hound starting to whimper again. I picked up the pace and walked faster even as briars began to jab through my pants and prick my legs. It was only a slight taste of the torture the dog was obviously enduring.

I found Edward just as I had left him. He heard the chomping of my footsteps through the foliage and turned to me, "Do you have it."

I wiped at my eyes with my free hand and choked out the word reluctantly, "Yes."

"Give it to me and go back to the truck." He didn't bother to stand, he just held out an open hand to me. His eyes were as full as mine and his face was already streaked with tears. I'd never held a gun before tonight and I'd never seen a grown man cry before. I handed him the pistol, but didn't go to the truck. I saw Edward stand and draw the gun before turning my head away. My fingers were quickly wedged tight into my ears.

Through plugged ears I could hear the sound of a two ton firecracker going off. I'm not sure what I thought would happen next, but I was surprised when Edward started to gently unwind the barbed wire from the hound. He took off is white linen shirt and wrapped it around the body. The shear respect Edward was giving this numb and lifeless canine far outweighed the consideration I'd ever seen Dwayne give any of the living ones.

I offered to help carry the body, but he shrugged me off. "I've got it, but thanks."

I nodded. "I'll clear a path for you." I took the lead this time. I held each branch safely out of the way for him to pass just as he had done for me. When we made it to the truck Edward asked me to open the back and he laid the body inside the back of the truck.

"Lucy, do you know how to drive?" Edward asked as he shut the tailgate. He took a moment just leaning against it. His hands were covered in blood and he just stared at them while waiting for my answer.

Every cell in my body shivered with sympathy for Edward. He reminded me of a shattered windowpane, damaged and dangerous to touch. I felt so helpless. What could I say or do? Delicately, I laid my hand on his shoulder. "I can drive."

Edward didn't budge and I felt compelled to wrap my arms around him. I slid my hand across his back from one shoulder to the other. He was a good bit taller than me, but his slumped posture was putting us almost cheek to cheek.

"I'm so sorry about all of this," I whispered and leaned my head against his.

"I've seen it done a hundred times before, but this is the first time I've had to do it. There's no way I could have gotten him to a vet in time. Hell, there's nothing a vet could have done."

"I know. I know."

"You don't hate me for doing it?" He barely turned his eyes toward me.

"I could never hate you. Sometimes, these things happen and you don't have a choice. He's better off now. No more suffering."

"Oh, Lucy, I'm so sorry for dragging you out here like this. I didn't know. If I had known..."

"Shhh." I pulled Edward closer to me. "I'm fine and there's no place I'd rather be." I honestly hated what had happened. But, I wouldn't have left him alone in that moment for anything in the world. Nothing mattered more than sharing this pain with him.

We stood there for a few minutes and the sounds of the forest were starting to return. It was dark now and there were more sounds than the gentle chirp of crickets and tree frogs I'd heard earlier. There was also the occasional howl of a coyote in the distance along with several other random rustlings closer to us.

"Come on. We'd better get going before folks start to wonder about us." I let go of Edward and started around toward the driver's side.

"Yeah," he tossed me the keys, "I promised to get you home and I don't want your mother to be worried or upset with me."

Chapter 6

"What are you going to do with him?" I asked Edward as I applied the brake to turn down the driveway to the hunt club. "The body, I mean."

I had three dogs in my life and one kitten. I played with them every day of their lives. One of the dogs ran away. One died of parvovirus as a puppy. Another lived to be twelve years old. The kitten choked to death on a piece of a hotdog that Mama accidentally dropped on the floor. All, but the one that ran away, were buried in our back yard. Mama and I held make-shift funerals for each one. She dug the hole and I said a prayer. I even painted rocks to serve as tombstones for them.

No one ever really played with the hounds. They served a purpose and now that this one had no purpose, I wondered what would happen to it. I figured it was unlikely to be buried in someone's back yard. In fact, this was the first one to die on my watch so I really didn't know what happened to them. It was a genuine question and mine were the first words spoken since I put the keys in the ignition. Unlike anyone else I'd ever been behind the wheel with, Edward didn't insist on criticizing my every move.

When he answered he didn't even bother lifting his head from where it was propped up by his elbow on the window sill. "There's a graveyard for them behind the kennel."

"Oh, I didn't know that." I'd never been any farther behind the kennel than the extensions of the fenced-in pavement. Knowing there was a graveyard for them made me feel better. I'm not sure what I thought would happen but knowing this little fella wouldn't just be thrown away made things just a slight bit less sad for me.

"I'll bury him back there after we get you home."

"I'll help you do it now if you like."

"It's getting late. I promised Lily I'd get you home and, like I said, we don't want your mother to worry."

"She won't worry. It's after 9:00 p.m. on a Wednesday and she's watching reruns of Party of Five."

Edward perked up. "Your mother watches Party of Five?"

"She discovered it about two weeks ago and can't seem to get enough. I think she's got a thing for Charlie."

"Really?"

"Yeah, I didn't see the whole episode, but one night something went on and Charlie cried and I caught my mother bawling, just bawling her eyes out. We both agreed that Charlie didn't have that ugly cry that most guys get."

I cut my eyes to Edward, suddenly self-conscious of what I had said since I had just seen him shed a few tears. I went ahead and pulled up in front of the kennel. I shut the engine off, but we didn't get out straight away.

"So what you're saying is that I have an ugly cry?" Edward was a good sport.

Joking or not, I was mortified. What was I to say? Answer truthfully and boldly tell him I thought he was perfect in every way, crying or not. Like Matthew Fox, the actor who played Charlie on the show, Edward looked great when he cried and it was endearing. I couldn't tell him that, but I couldn't insult him either.

"No offense, I really wasn't focused on you then."

"Well good. I don't normally..."

"It's okay. I do normally cry when animals suffer." I explained to him about life at Nanny and Papa's. "It wasn't an everyday occurrence, but when Papa had to do it, it was sad. I think anyone with a heart would think it was sad."

"I think you're right."

Edward grabbed a shovel and I grabbed the flashlight and in the dark he dug the hole while I held the light. At the end of it we said a prayer and Edward took me home. He even walked me to the door and, depressing as it was, that beat out the trip to the movies and fighting off Maggie's cousin Kevin for being the closest thing to a first date I'd ever had.

I shut the front door and fell against it. Mama was right where I knew she would be. It was nearing ten, the last five minutes of the show, and she shushed me when I closed the door. I only rested there for a second before I turned and ran back out to catch Edward. He had the truck in reverse and was backing out of the driveway, but I managed to get his attention and he pulled back in.

Over the sound of the motor, I shouted, "What are you doing Saturday night?"

Edward raised an eyebrow. He thought I was asking him out. I blushed and quickly clarified my question. "I mean, if you're not doing anything else, then I thought, maybe you could come to my birthday party. It's nothing big."

"I'll see what I can do."

"Okay. Well, goodnight, again."

"Goodnight, Green."

"Goodnight, Edward."

Thursday at the kennel was uneventful. As what was the norm now, Dwayne sulked over my riding lessons and he was even more put out by me having been invited out with the hunt. He made snide comments to me about being one of them.

"Some of us have to do the heavy lifting, but others of us are just here for decoration," he said as he picked up one of the dogs and threw it out of his way.

I ignored what he said, but went and checked on the dog that landed up against the back cinderblock wall. This was just another example of how he treated the dogs on a daily basis and I was tired of it. After what I had witnessed on Wednesday night, I knew they had feelings. I saw the eyes of the one that Edward put down as it lay dying. They deserved compassion in their day to day lives, not just on Wednesdays when they caught a fox or coyote or when they were dying. I decided I was going to say something to him. I didn't know when and I didn't know how, but I was going to do it.

Friday afternoon I was throwing out the last bucket of chicken when Dwayne came along. "Lucy, Mrs. Pope wants you to come with me and check the gates."

In the few weeks that I had been there we'd never gone and checked gates before so I should have known something was up, but my intuition radar was on the fritz. Edward had walked down that morning and accepted the invitation to my party. I was turning sixteen the next day and I was over the moon. I didn't think to question Dwayne at all.

I climbed into the cab of his truck and away we went. He made an immediate right out of the drive. If one was headed toward town the road forked in a curve right in front of the driveway to the hunt club. I had never noticed the name of the road, but Dwayne turned onto it. He went at least a half mile down the road and then he made a left onto another of the tire track roads.

I tried to say something to him about how he treated the hounds, but he just turned the radio up so loud I couldn't hear myself think.

Far into the woods we went. I did my best to take notice of each turn we took and landmarks. I counted at least three gates that he made me get out and open and four different times we turned from one set of tire tracks onto the other. We passed an old home place where only a chimney and a lean-to barn were still standing. We passed countless deer stands and went through a grove of pecan trees. We drove along the edge of a pond and along the dam before turning onto another road that split the woods.

I looked behind us a number of times to try to remind myself of what we'd passed, but, all in all, by the time Dwayne stopped the truck, I was lost. Excitement for my birthday vanished and it was replaced with concern. We hadn't checked any gates. We had only gone deeper and deeper into the woods with me opening one after another.

The radio still blared and Dwayne made no move to get out. I looked from side to side and front and back.

"I really need to be getting back. My mother's picking me up early today and she doesn't like to be kept waiting." That was a lie. She didn't like to be kept waiting, but she wasn't coming after me early. The truth was, I was afraid. There was no one for miles and I was keenly aware of that. Edward's warning was now echoing in my ears.

It happened in a matter of seconds. The truck lurched to a stop. My heart began racing, as Dwayne lunged for me inside the cab. His truck was an automatic so there was no gear shift to slow him down. His full weight was pressed against me and I was firmly backed into the passenger side door. The feeling of panic was like having hands clenched around my throat. Was I still breathing? I remember thinking that this could not possibly be happening for real. But, sadly it was quite real. Almost more real than I could handle.

Dwayne's S-10 pick-up was a tight fit for two people and even a tighter squeeze for what was becoming painfully clear were his intended activities. For a second, the shock of it kept me from fighting him off. I clenched my eyes tight and saw Edward's face inside my head. This was a runt of a truck compared to Edward's full size Bronco and Dwayne was a runt of a man, a weasel who was stealing a kiss. A hand up my leg and digging at my shorts, gave indication that he aimed at stealing much more. I'd never imagined.

I came to my senses and the fight was on.

I twisted my face away from him and shoved him as much as I could. "Get off me!" I screamed in a voice straight from the bowels of Hell.

"Look here!" I was surprised when Dwayne grabbed a wadded handful of my shirt, right at the seam where the sleeve and body met, and jerked me back to him. My neck whipped and I slammed into his chest. He shook me and bounced my head off of the glass of the window. It was a blinding blow, but I heard it clearly.

"I hear you like it in the woods." There was grinding of his teeth and growling in his voice. He thought he had me.

With a thud he kissed me for the second time. My first kiss had been stolen from me, but the second one he'd pay dearly for. My knee slammed squarely into his groin. The blow didn't help in getting him off of me. It only helped him fall limp as I fought with all I was worth. While he scrambled to keep hold of me and his balls at the same time, I got in a good scratch to his face with one hand. I reached for my door handle with the other, and pulled it hard and fast. The door flung open and I toppled out to the ground.

"You white-trash bitch!" Dwayne clawed after me, trying desperately to keep hold of me. I might have been winded from falling flat on my back in the dirt, but I was free.

I got to my feet and he was still flopping about on his belly half out of the truck. I got around the door and kicked it shut. Dwayne saw it coming and just barely got out of the way as the door rattled the hinges.

I didn't stick around to see what he was going to do next. I ran. I had enough wits about me to run off the side of the beaten down tracks and into the woods. At that point, I didn't put it past Dwayne to mow me down with the truck if I stayed in the open.

Briars thrashing at my legs, I could feel the slicing, cutting, prickling of the thorns, but I kept running. I jumped over fallen trees like an Olympic hurdler. I forgot watching where I put my feet and looking out for snakes. I just ran.

From a distance I heard him revving the engine and the whine it made when he floored it in reverse. In the distance I heard him grind the gears when he found a spot to turn around and kept going. I ran until I couldn't hear the truck anymore. I didn't trust him not to come back.

When Dwayne was long out of range for me to hear him, I stopped and I dropped my head between my knees and panted. My heart raced, beating nearly out of my chest. I'd never ran that far or that fast before. It took a minute before I could catch my breath enough to assess my surroundings.

In every distance there was nothing but pines. I looked to the sky for the sun to get my bearings. The sun sets in the west, but all I could see were tree tops. They let in just enough light to give me a hint. As best I could figure, town was southeast and the hunt club was four miles outside of town. If I just kept walking toward town maybe I would come back out on the road closer it. That was my plan. I would just keep walking until I came to a main road and then I would walk to someone's house. It was still daylight and what choice did I have? No one knew where I was. I had to walk back.

For the first hour I walked and wondered what Dwayne would say happened to me. I didn't have a car so I couldn't have driven off on my own. What did he think I would say when I turned back up?

The second hour, when I still hadn't made it to a main road, I began to think he didn't mean for me to make it back. My imagination started to run away with me.

Nanny had wild dogs that sometimes came around her property. What if there were wild dogs out here? I knew there were coyotes in the area. I was told the hounds got the scent of one and chased it two weeks ago when the hunt went out on Sunday afternoon. Wild dogs and coyotes, that's all I could think about and rustling bushes that sounded like animals in the woods didn't help.

Finally, I realized I'd made a circle. I noticed the same forked tree and the skinned spot where lightening had struck it. I was too far around to go back so I kept walking.

I finally came to another of what I would call a logging road. Unlike the road Edward and I went down to find the hound, this one was not completely lost to nature. It appeared to be used regularly as there was no brush growing in the middle between the tire tracks. The road made enough of a clearing that I could see the sun. I could make out which way was north, south, east and west. The road had two options east or west and I chose east.

I looked at my watch and it was nearing 5:00 p.m. Mama would be there to get me soon. Dwayne would have to explain. Or would he? He left before me last week. I stopped and started to cry. No one would be there to tell my mother where I was. No one would know where to look for me. I felt utterly hopeless and terrified. Dogs and coyotes, I couldn't shake the thought of them either and that didn't help.

I tried to keep walking, but I could hardly see through my tears. I struggled to put one foot in front of the other. I had never wanted to see my mother so badly in my entire life.

Another thirty minutes I went on crying and walking, walking and crying and then I got the strange sensation that I was being followed. It was more than the wind blowing through the underbrush of the forest. This was the sound of four light footed steps that caused the hair on the back of my neck to stand up.

I turned back to see, but my eyes were puffy and blurred. I couldn't make out what it was, but it was big. Any other day I would have known better than to run, but not today, I panicked and ran. I ran as fast as I could, which wasn't very fast at all. I was exhausted from walking, but I ran like a third string track team sprinter, all effort, but no real speed. Sure enough, the big furry blob behind me gave chase.

A ringing rattling sound mixed with the huffing of its breath came after me. It caught me with little to no effort. I was only a few paces ahead of it when I glanced back to check the distance between us and I tripped and fell. I just knew I was about to be the lead actress in a bad horror movie. I went face down into the dirt while praying and covering my head.

My prayers were answered by a Collie dog licking my ear when I rolled over. The rattling and clanking noise was his collar. He had a little silver bone on the collar with, "Barker Hobbs" and a phone number inscribed on it.

I met Mr. and Mrs. Hobbs at the hunt on Wednesday night. They mentioned that they lived close-by, so close that their old dog often wandered down to the kennel on a hunt of his own.

"A hunt for a girlfriend among the bitches," Mr. Hobbs snickered.

They called the female hounds "bitches" and no one blinked an eye over it, no one but me.

The sweet beast now slobbering all over me was definitely Mr. and Mrs. Hobbs' dog and that meant their house must be nearby.

I acted just like Timmy's mom from Lassie and begged Barker to lead me home. "Oh please, please help me."

My feet and legs ached from walking. I was tired. I had been wandering around in the woods for almost three hours. It was past time for my mother to pick me up. I could hear sirens in the distance. I didn't know if they were coming to make a report on my disappearance or what.

A disappearance would be quite the scandal for Thomson. No one ever went missing from here. I kicked at the sand and kept walking, Barker at my side. I didn't want the missing person to be me. Maybe the sirens were for some other reason. Maybe they were just for the usual Friday afternoon wreck in front of the BiLo. Nanny always complained about the treachery, her word, of driving on the old four-lane in Friday afternoon traffic.

"I'd rather get groceries in Augusta at midnight, than get them here on a Friday afternoon. Ain't no carton of eggs that important and, if they're gonna expire by 5:30 p.m. on Friday, then I don't want 'em anyway." Thinking of Nanny made me cry even more. If only Mr. Watson had left well enough alone, I wouldn't be tromping around in the woods wondering if I'd ever see my grandmother again.

I sniffed back the draining byproduct of my tears and kept walking. I was certain this was the road to depression, mental illness and ultimately the road to Hell. For me, the road was paved with the good intentions of Boyd Watson and I didn't even know why.

I regretted the decision I made when all of this started. I regretted agreeing to this job at the kennel. I regretted so many things now including not going back out of the woods the same direction Dwayne had gone, but I was too deep in to turn back now. Plus, I'm not sure I would remember all of the turns. Who's to say I wouldn't be just as lost.

I pondered those things and whether I would get out before dark. I was starting to panic over the thought of not making it out and being found before dark when Barker started to run ahead of me. Tears were in my eyes again, but through them I could see the trees thinning out. In the trees I could see the back of a house and a truck.

I called up every bit of strength left in my legs and I ran as fast as I could to the house. It was a brick ranch, similar to our house, but much larger. It had a two car garage instead of a one car, but there was a door under the carport, just like our house. It was the first door I saw and I banged on it as if my life depended on it.

Mrs. Hobbs called through the door, "Who is it?"

"It's Lucy Meeks from the hunt club."

I wasn't even halfway through telling Mrs. Hobbs what had happened when she loaded me into her Cadillac and squalled the tires. Straight to the club we went. She was fuming over Dwayne's actions.

"That boy's been nothing but trouble from the word go. You know what happened to his hand?" she asked as she took to the pavement on two wheels.

"Yes, ma'am."

"I'm sure your mother is sick with worry! I knew your daddy and I'm telling you, the man I knew before he went to Vietnam, would have beat the cold livin' shit out of anyone that messed with his family. Dwayne better be glad your dad's not here to teach him a lesson. Heck, if I tell Benny, he's liable to do the job himself."

Benny was Mr. Hobbs and I was pretty sure she was going to tell him. If he did give Dwayne the beating of his life, I would be glad of it.

Mama's car, Mr. Watson's car, Mrs. Pope's truck and several other vehicles including three sheriff's department cars were in the yard of the kennel. Mr. Watson had his arm around Mama and they were talking to one of the deputies. Two other deputies were milling around and Edward was standing out in front of the kennel with them. I'd never been so happy to see all of them in my whole life. I never thought I would see any of them again.

Mrs. Hobbs' car wasn't even stopped when I threw open the door and jumped out. I ran to Mama and she ran to me. It was like a scene from a cheesy romantic comedy movie, except it was two women running into one another's arms. Mr. Watson was right behind her and I was so happy to see them that I didn't even mind his interference.

Mama's face was streaked with the remains of black rivers from her eyes to her neck. If only she would get on board with waterproof mascara, but she wouldn't give up the stuff she'd been using since the seventies.

Maggie's dad was there. Edward was there and over Mama's shoulder, I could see he was pacing. His hands were clenched and, although he was talking to Mr. McCorkle and the Master of the Hounds, he didn't take his eyes off of me. The men looked to one another and Edward as they spoke, the way folks do when they are carrying on a conversation, but not Edward. I could see him over Mama's shoulders. All I could think was he warned me and he was mad with me for not listening or my intuition. In fact, my intuition radar went off. I was too excited about tomorrow to think about anything else.

I leaned back from Mama and she held my face in her hands. "If you ever scare me like that again, I swear I will beat you!"

I looked over her to Edward and caught him still watching me. "I'm fine. No harm done. Just a little scare and some sore legs from walking for so long."

I hadn't really noticed until then, but Mr. Watson was hugging me right along with Mama.

"This could have ended so much worse." Mr. Watson paused and turned around from us. He ran his hand through his hair and exhaled in a huge sigh of relief. "What were you doing in woods?"

I thought I had taken note of everyone that was out there, but I looked around to make sure. I didn't see Dwayne. Ten or more people standing around waiting to find out where I had been, but he wasn't one of them. Not finding him lurking around made it easier to tell exactly what happened.

"Dwayne told me that Mrs. Pope wanted us to check on some gates," I began.

Mrs. Pope interjected, "I never!" She shook her head. "That wouldn't be a part of your job."

Mr. Watson waived her off so I could continue. "Go on, Lucy."

"He drove me way back in the woods. I lost track of how many turns, four, or five. I'm not sure. Then, he stopped." I went on to tell them about how he kissed me.

I glanced at Edward. I didn't want to repeat exactly what Dwayne said to me in front of him, what he said about me liking it in the woods. It was an implication about the evening with Edward when the hound died. There was nothing likeable about the circumstances surrounding that night and the only thing that went on with me and Edward that night was bonding over the loss of that dog. We bonded over common decency and now Dwayne had done his best to tarnish that, but I wouldn't let him.

The white haired deputy, the senior of the three who was taking notes and asking the majority of the questions that Mama and Mr. Watson weren't asking, saved me having to give every detail. "So Miss, he assaulted you and kidnapped you?"

I hadn't thought of it like that before. To me that was a strong word. I could feel my facial expression change as I contemplated the answer. I suppose the look on my face was answer enough.

"Get a car over to that boy's house and bring him back here," Deputy Phillips nodded toward one of the others.

"Yes, sir." The deputy sprinted to his car. He didn't even ask any of us if we knew where Dwayne lived. I guess they knew from their prior dealings with him over the mailbox bombings.

As the dust flung up every which way and the deputy sped away, Mama distracted me from watching. She asked the question on everyone's mind. It was on their faces, the fright in their eyes and pity for me. They wanted to know.

"Baby." I couldn't remember the last time she called me baby. She pulled my head over to her shoulder and leaned her head against mine. "Did he rape you?"

"No!" I was adamant.

Chapter 7

Mama continued to fret over me and that was an action and emotion that was foreign to both of us. I was keenly aware of that, but she was oblivious. The whole ordeal, from the time I got in the truck with Dwayne earlier until right that very second, was uncomfortable. I'd never had so many people, including her, focused on me in my entire life.

I hated Dwayne for leaving me in the woods, but his timing for maximum damage on my life couldn't have been more perfect. This was steadily becoming a black cloud that was going to hang over my sixteenth birthday. Years from now I wouldn't remember what I wore to my party, but I would remember the day that, as the deputy put it, I was kidnapped and assaulted. The day wasn't even here yet, but I knew he had ruined it. He hadn't been invited to the party, but he'd be there just the same, the memory of what he'd done to me and the pestering question of it I had lied about how much he might have assaulted me would be on everyone's minds. Even though I was telling the truth, I could see the doubt in my mother's eyes. I could see the doubt in all of their eyes.

Mama looked me up and down. My knees were skinned and my clothes were all kinds of disheveled. My shorts were ripped and I there were salt lines from the sweat-stains around the sleeves of my t-shirt. My face was puffy from crying. I knew I looked like I had been through the ringer. All of that could be explained away and it didn't include me being raped.

The stares from all of them were starting to weigh on me. I just wanted to go home and I begged my mother and she looked to the chief deputy.

"Why not?" Mr. Watson interjected. He had yet to release my mother's hand. For once, the two of them made no secret that there was something more between them than employer and employee.

"We'll want to see what the boy has to say, plus..."

"What does it matter what *he* has to say? Lucy told you what happened and that should be enough!"

Mr. Watson wasn't thinking much like a lawyer according to the deputy.

As the officer and Mr. Watson went at it, Edward finally approached and pulled me away. He was a welcome distraction. Pulling me away freed Mama from hanging and hugging all over me and allowed her to get between Mr. Watson and the deputy. Mr. Watson had let go of Mama's hand by then and had doubled his fists. They were still at his sides when Edward got my attention, but I could tell it might come to blows.

"Are you alright?" Edward asked in the same voice I'd heard him use to comfort the dying hound the other night.

I could hardly take my eyes off of his hand still entwined with mine. He had a lone mole, one of the flat kind, more like a big freckle than a mole, on the center of his back of his hand. Other than that, his hands were so smooth and tan, so tan that the veins weren't as visible in his as they were in my pale hand.

Edward had simply taken my hand to get my attention and guided me away from my mother. We'd stepped some ten feet from Mama and the other gentleman, but he still had his fingers locked gently in mine. How strange it seemed that that small touch from him was more comforting to me than all of the hugs Mama had just given me.

"I'm fine." I barely raised my eyes to his.

"You're lying," he leaned closer to me and whispered in my ear. "Did he..."

I didn't let Edward finish the question. "No!" I answered plainly. "I'm not lying. He tried but he didn't succeed. He just scared the life out of me is all."

I turned my head from Edward because I didn't want him looking at me and pitying me and I certainly didn't want him thinking that Dwayne had taken, well, I just didn't want him to think that had happened to me. The thing was, if Dwayne had done that to me, I would be screaming from the rooftops for him to suffer.

"Are you..."

I stopped Edward again. "The scrapes on my legs are from where I ran through briars and where I fell and skinned them when the Hobbs' dog chased me and I fell. My shorts, again courtesy of the briars, and I probably have a big bruise on my behind from where I fell out of the truck and landed in the dirt. Now, please don't ask me anything else. I'm really trying not to cry again."

Edward gave me just enough of a tug that I fell into his arms. "Bury your face and cry all you want." He whispered over the top of my head. For a moment there was no one else around but the two of us.

I tried not to cry, but I felt the moisture slip down my cheeks even though his arms around me was just what I needed and I hadn't even known it.

"If they bring him back up here I'll beat the shit out of him if he even looks your way." My head was snug beneath his chin and as he spoke he stroked the back of my neck.

Although I wasn't a fan of violence, I wouldn't be opposed to him teaching Dwayne a lesson about messing with me. I also tried not to read anything into his gesture or words other than that he was only being nice to me.

When I finally backed up from Edward what little of my make up that was left after my earlier crying fits was now smeared on his shirt. He always had on the same white Polo shirt and tan riding pants. I guess it was what he considered a uniform for work. I had seen him outside of work twice so I knew he had more clothes. Thinking about his wardrobe kept my mind occupied while we waited for the deputy to return with Dwayne.

I clutched my hands around him and held him as he did me. The shirt was softer than I had imagined. It was the dream of every fabric softener manufacturer to create clothes this soft. And, the way he smelled. I had never been so close that my nose touched him, touched heaven before.

Edward tried to distract me further and to keep me from hearing the conversations of the adults. They were all standing in a circle with Mr. Hobbs and Maggie's dad both offering to take care of the problem for Mr. Watson. I didn't see how it was his problem. I didn't dwell on that too much, but I was curious.

"So you invited me to your party, but I don't remember you giving me any details," Edward prodded.

Keeping my eyes on Mr. Watson, his arm around Mama, who at this point was more shaken than I was, I tried to hear what was being said. His fists were unclenched, but his jaw was still tight. I couldn't hear them and I didn't want to be rude so I turned my attention back to him.

"It was supposed to be at the Thomson Country Club where my grandfather has a membership, but Mr. Watson sold Mama on the idea of having it at the Half-way house. I don't know what the Half-way house is, but she said he could get it for free and free was a big deal to her. Anything Mr. Watson says is a big deal to her." I kicked at the dirt and was reminded just how far I had walked and ran that afternoon. My muscles ached to the bone.

Edward placed his hand at the small of my back. "Walk with me."

He led me over to the fence that outlined the pasture behind the hunt barn. He propped his elbows up on the top rail of the fence and pointed toward the far end of the stable. "See that group of trees across the road?"

The only trees across the road were up the road and across not just across so it took me a minute to spot what he was talking about. I was looking for something a little closer than a half mile away.

"In the middle of those pecan trees," Edward went on as he adjusted his posture, putting a foot up on the bottom rung, "is an old house. You've seen it before. That's the place they call the Half-way house."

He was right. I had seen it before. I'd even been inside once when Mr. Watson and Lily lived there for two weeks while the kitchen was being remodeled at their house.

"It's old, but I like it. I like old things." He kept staring in the distance at the house.

With my shoulder I nudged him in the side and gave him a sideways glance. "I like old things too."

I forgot about my afternoon for a second and flirted with Edward. I'd never been so bold before.

Edward cut his eyes at me and smiled with a slight chuckle. After that there was nothing but the sound of summer, the animals that were beginning to stir as dusk approached and the chatter from the grown folks. Edward and I just leaned on the fence.

I could distinctly feel each spot where our bodies touched, neither of us backing away. I was either leaning into him or he was leaning into me, I'm not sure which, but my waist pressed into his hip and we were almost glued together along the sides of our thighs. My shoulder still rested on is arm from where I had nudged him. I looked up and down at the seam our arms made and as I did chill bumps from the thrill of him not backing away sprang up all over my arm, both arms.

"Lucy..."

"I like it when you call me Green."

Edward shook his head and before a single other word could be uttered, our attention was drawn to the return of the car that carried the deputy away to find Dwayne.

I felt my chest heave and I caught my breath. Edward noticed and took my hand again. My heart raced as much as the speeding patrol car did.

"No one's going to let him near you," in my ear Edward assured me.

We waited where we were and watched as the deputy emerged from the car. He strode toward the group and Deputy Phillips met him halfway. I couldn't hear a word, but the body language could be heard by all of us.

Deputy Phillips slung his hat from his head and beat it about his leg with distinct disappointment as the other one, the one that had been sent to fetch Dwayne, threw up his hands and shook his head.

"They didn't find Dwayne." I looked back at Edward and I could tell he knew it too. "You think he's on the run or something?"

The long and short of it was that Dwayne Richards was tin the wind, a real scoundrel who had for all appearances skipped town in the hours while I was wandering in the woods. Mr. Watson didn't mix words with his description of Dwayne and in his opinion the word "scoundrel" didn't do him justice. Mama, who was not one to throw around the curse words, especially in public, didn't hold back with her use of the word "bastard."

"A real cowardly bastard!" those were her exact words.

As much as Dwayne was a bastard, Mr. Watson was an enigma. After everyone cleared out, the deputies to get warrants for his arrest and put out an A.P.B. on Dwayne, Mr. McCorkle had to go and get Maggie from Camp Fulton so she would be home for my party the following night and Mr. and Mrs. Hobbs had to get back home for Mrs. Hobbs to cut off the crockpot, Mr. Watson suggested that Mama and I join him and Lily for dinner in Augusta. As he was inviting Mama and I, Edward was saying his good-byes so Mr. Watson asked him to join us.

"Let's go to the Olive Garden. You girls up for it?" Mr. Watson was clearly doing his best to brighten everyone's mood.

Mama shook her head and declined. "Not tonight, Boyd."

Public displays of affection and concern all afternoon, nothing so grand as a kiss, but they were slipping. She even called him by his first name and didn't bother to correct herself and he didn't flinch. Watching them I got the impression that he might not care what she called him as long as she called.

"Mary, be serious. Y'all've got to eat and there's no way you're going home to cook now." He wasn't pushy or demanding as I'd usually seen him. He was persuasive and the way he caressed his hand across the back of her neck, he genuinely cared for her.

"Plus," noticing my eyes wide with wonder over them, he backed off, "I'm not sure it's a good idea for you all to go home alone with this boy on the loose."

"I'll go," Edward said and seemed to pep up.

A look passed between Edward and Mr. Watson. Edward clearly agreed about us not going home alone.

I tugged at Mama as Mr. Watson backed off. "Let's go. You know the Olive Garden's your favorite."

Before Mama could balk again Mr. Watson expressed his delight. "Great! It's settled," pulling his keys from his pocket he started for his car. "You can drop your car at my house and we'll pick-up Lily at the same time. Edward, you want ride with me?"

"Sure, I just need a minute to change if you don't mind." Edward slapped at his pants dusting them off.

Mr. Watson nodded in acceptance and Edward headed off to the apartment above the barn.

I glanced down at my own situation. I was in more need of a change than any of the rest of them including Edward. There was still dried blood streaked down one of my shins from where I had skinned my knee.

Mama started toward our car. I called to her, "Mama?"

She glanced back to me as she opened the car door.

"I can't go to dinner looking like this."

Mama looked me over head to toe. Her eyes became glassy with tears springing up. She gave a slight acknowledgment and dabbed her eyes with her fingertips. "Go ahead and get in the car. I'll be right back."

The truth was neither of us looked fit for dinner out. We didn't even look fit for dinner in. We have been put through the ringer.

Mama returned in a few minutes.

"We're going to wait and Edward's going to come to the house with us while Boyd picks up Lily then they'll come get us." Mama smiled reassurance that everything was going to be alright.

Our house was fine. There's wasn't a blade of grass out of place in the yard or a cock-eyed picture on the wall or one snippet of dust out of place in the whole house. Thing were as they should be, except Edward was inside, sitting in my spot on the couch watching MTV while Mama and I took turns in the bathroom.

Mama emerged looking like the beauty queen she once was and I did the best with what I had. I choose a long flowing skirt to cover the wounds to my knees and a tank top. I scrubbed in the shower as memories of the struggle with Dwayne haunted me. I couldn't shake that he'd stolen my first kiss. I knew I should be grateful that was all he stole and I was. The problem was that I had fantasized since the day I had first seen him that my first kiss would be given to Edward.

It was 8:00 p.m. on the nose when Mr. Watson pulled up with Lily. He drove an older Mercedes, the kind with the hump still in the middle. On the hump is where Edward rode, the middle of the back seat with one leg on one side of the floor board and another on the other side. He was every bit of six foot one with his knees drawn up to his chin just about, but he volunteered for that spot so Mama could have the front seat. I tried to get him to switch with me,

125

but so did Lily. It was obvious Lily and I were such children both wanting to sit next to Edward.

Lily, Edward and I were crammed in the back seat, but there was enough room on the seat between our legs that I rested my hand on the leather. I gazed out of the window trying not to think about Dwayne Richards and where he might be, trying not to think about anything at all.

One hand was in his lap and another rested on the seat between us, rested next to mine. Our hands started off about two inches apart, but slowly, with each bump in the road, they slipped closer. I could see them in my peripheral vision, but I didn't dare look square on at them for fear if I looked Edward might move back or Lily might notice. I held my hand as still as I held my head. I let him come to me and the anticipation of his touch sent butterflies scattering about my belly.

Lily went on and on in an attempt to hold a complete conversation with Edward. We were hardly onto the main road toward Augusta before Lily started in with Edward. I listened, but didn't participate. I just kept watch of the white line on the edge of the road.

No doubt Mr. Watson had told Lily what had happened to me that afternoon, but, if he did, she gave no inclination of it. She didn't mention one word on the subject. The most she said to me was "good evening" and the little protest she gave about which of us would sit in the middle. Other than that, she was all about Edward. I can't say as I blamed her.

"Tell me again about how you're related to the Queen of England," Lily fawned over him.

"It's nothing, really."

"Oh come on. How far in the succession line?"

I heard them, but, more importantly, I felt his hand brush against mine as he answered Lily. "I'm 56th in line for the throne."

"So, if this were like during the time of the War of the Roses, then you'd have to kill fifty-five people before you could be King Edward."

"Yes, Lily, thirty-five people and including my father." Edward slipped his pinky finger under mine and my eyes fluttered.

"Didn't you tell me you were named after...?"

"Yes, after King Edward IV. It's on my father's side, but my mother has always been far more interested in the family history and association than he has ever been. I guess we're all glad she wasn't blessed with more sons. Instead of brothers named George and Richard or a wife named Elizabeth, I have sisters named Isabella and Anne." Edward was smart with his remarks, pestered by Lily, but patronized her anyway. Anyone could hear in his voice that he was annoyed.

Lily laughed. "I think it's fascinating. She named them after the wives of the brothers instead."

I rolled my eyes. It's not that I didn't want to know more about Edward, but I really didn't need a history lesson right then. What I needed was peace and quiet.

With each jarring of the old Mercedes, our hands touched ever so slightly more. My breath caught with every rock, crack and divot in the road. I just wanted quiet so I could be lost in his touch.

Edward broke the conversation and turned his full attention to me for a split second. "You can prop against me if you like. I don't mind. I know you're tired." Over my shoulder I gave him a sleepy smile and a squeeze to his hand. I leaned back from the window and laid softly into him. I didn't see Lily's face, but there was a huff in the air from her direction. I closed my eyes and remembered her warning from my first few days at the kennel.

"Don't get any ideas."

Chapter 8

Ideas.

What sort of ideas was it that I wasn't supposed to get? Lily was clear, I wasn't supposed to get any ideas about Edward. She'd been clear about that since before I met him.

Was I not supposed to get any ideas about Mama and Mr. Watson? They carried on a private conversation, low and casual, all the way to the restaurant. In one regard I was a million miles away, but in another I heard the hum of all that was going on in the car.

I had slept from the time I leaned back into Edward which was around Harlem, the rest of Gordon Highway was a blur. I'm not sure if Mr. Watson zigzagged around Highland Avenue and then along the side of Augusta National or if he took Bobby Jones to Washington Road. All I knew is that I woke up at the Olive Garden.

I glanced around the table at the restaurant. The table was round and next to me on one side was Mama, then Mr. Watson, Lily, Edward and then me again. Again, the seating was mostly orchestrated by Lily. If she could have figured out a way to sit Mama between Edward and me without being obvious, I think she would have.

I was no competition for conversation so Lily ruled. I was blurry eyed through most of dinner, still half asleep from the ride over. I picked at my salad and then did more of the same with my pasta. Normally, I could kill three breadsticks from The Olive Garden all the while mopping up my salad dressing with them, but not tonight. I hardly ate a bite.

The inquisition continued from Lily about Edward and his relation to the "Queen's Country". Finally, he'd had enough.

"Honestly," he said with restrained sincerity, "I moved away from there when I was little more than a toddler."

Mr. Watson gave her that nod he was famous for, the signal that she's said enough on the subject. I glanced at her and she was clearly embarrassed, red faced and treated like a child not a young woman of twenty. She lacked the social training of those of us who'd attended school with others all of our lives. She'd been doted on and isolated so much that now she came across as obnoxious in group settings. To make matters worse, her father treated her like a child and hadn't let go an inch.

Lily's intentions toward Edward were becoming more and more obvious to me. Despite her frailty, despite her childlike ways, despite everything, she was still a young woman. She might not have known how to woo a man any more than I did, but she wanted to try.

It was after 9:00 p.m. and the whole restaurant was still a buzz. I was lost with my thoughts, my ideas. The handholding from Edward came rushing back to me.

Mr. Watson changed the conversation to the subject of my pending birthday. "Only about three more hours until the big day." His appetite hadn't suffered at all. One forkful on top of the other and he was talking about ordering dessert at the same time.

Mama grinned. "It's more like nine hours to go. Lucy was born at 6:10 a.m. and she weighed six pounds ten ounces and had a head full of hair." She reached over and tussled my curls.

I ducked out of her hand. "Mama, stop," I protested.

"She had the dimples even then," added Mr. Watson.

"You were there that night?" My question directed to Mr. Watson.

"And she was so cubby," Lily continued as if I hadn't said a word.

"Luckily, I grew out of that," politely I nodded. "Mr. Watson..."

"I think it's about time you called me Boyd and, yes, I was there the night you were born."

"Why?" I felt the word slip from my lips, but it wasn't my voice I heard. It was Lily's.

Mr. Watson, Boyd, whatever, he looked at Lily and again she received a couple of stinging daggers. "Yes. I was there that night."

Lily fell silent and Edward picked up the torch. "How long have you two worked together?"

Mama joined in. "Since he opened the doors of his practice. Let me think." She dabbed the corners of her mouth with her napkin before looking to Mr. Watson. "Was that 1977?"

Mr. Watson gave a confirming shake of his head. "Mary and my wife were best friends in high school."

"You were?" I was surprised. No one ever mentioned Mr. Watson's wife. She was much like some mythical creature that only left hints of her actual existence, kind of like the Lock Ness Monster.

"Yes," Mama acknowledged.

Edward did my work for me. "I don't mean to pry, but what happened to her?"

This conversation had definitely perked me up. Three sentences, this was the most we'd ever spoken about Mrs. Watson. It was remarkable because everyone seemed at ease with the subject.

Mr. Watson took a sip of his wine, but he answered. "She died right about the time Lucy was born."

I thought it and I said it. "I never knew. How? I mean, what..."

"She had cancer. Lily comes by it honest." He gave her a warming smile.

"That's about all I got from her. Everything else about me is Daddy through and through, nose, hair, legs of a chicken." Lily made a joke at his expense and he didn't shoot her down. Maybe he had a sense of humor after all.

"Yes, chicken legs and all," he agreed.

I had never taken a real good look at them before and studied their features. They did look a great deal alike and that was funny to me considering tons of people had commented that Lily and I looked alike. We were mistaken for sisters on more than a few occasions.

I cut my eyes from Lily to Mr. Watson to Mama and I put those ideas out of my head.

I hardly slept that night. Mr. Watson left Edward to sleep on our couch. Mama objected at first, but what Boyd Watson wanted, Boyd Watson got. It was funny even though I put the thoughts of Mr. Watson and Mama out of my head, we all functioned like a family that night, a family with two houses. I knew there was a budding rivalry between me and Lily, a sisterly rivalry over a boy. I wasn't sure of Edward's place in the family, but he seemed a fixture in it this summer just like Mama and I were.

The clock said 3:22 a.m. That was the last time I looked at it. From the time I went to bed at nearly midnight until then, I dreamed in blocks of twenty minute intervals, like twenty minutes on twenty minutes off. I would sleep then jolt to life with a gasp only to do it all over again. I tossed and turned, stuck my head under the pillow, cut the fan on, cut it off and a number of other things to try to get past scary vignettes of Dwayne Richards that played in my head.

It was a nice change to sleep with the air conditioner on, but I knew the only reason Mama sprang for the extra expense of the electricity was so that we could shut the windows and lock them. When I gave up on sleeping, I had to pull the spread over me to venture to the kitchen. The house was unusually cold for late June.

A glass of milk, a piece of cheese, I stood in the refrigerator looking for something, but I wasn't sure what. I heard the rustling in the living room and remembered Edward was camping out in there. I closed the refrigerator and tiptoed over to the couch.

It was darker than dark in there, but my eyes had adjusted enough for me to see his outline under the blanked strewn from one of the end of the couch to the other. His feet were handing off the corner at one end. He was entirely too big to be comfortable on our tiny couch.

"Edward," I squatted next to his head on the couch and whispered. "Are you asleep?"

Groggy and half lying, he replied, "No."

I went from just squatting to sitting on my knees on the floor next to him.

"You can't sleep?" He shifted to his side and faced me.

Even as just a shadow, Edward was one of God's miracles to look at.

I shrugged my shoulders. "Uh-uh." I yawned. "Every time I drift off, it's like I am back in the woods again. I never minded the woods before, but now," I exhaled.

"It's okay."

"I'm sorry I didn't listen to you." I dropped my head into the cushion and buried my face.

"What do you mean?" Edward laid a hand over the back of my head and ran his fingers through my hair.

"I didn't heed your warning about Dwayne this afternoon and I know none of this would have happened if..."

Edward scooted around on the couch so that he was in a positon to lift my chin. "Hey, this isn't your fault. Some boys are made for doing bad things and he's one of them and they're not good for much else. Dwayne's one of those kinds of boys. Just because you trust someone doesn't mean when they break your trust that it's your fault. You understand?"

"Why are you so nice to me?"

Edward didn't answer the question. "Here," he rose from the couch, "You take it and I'll sleep right down here." He motioned to the spot on the floor where I'd been sitting.

"What? No. I'll go back to bed. It's alright." I extended a hand and offered him the couch back.

"Take the couch, Green."

Reluctantly, I crawled onto the couch while Edward rearranged the covers Mama had given him. He made a pallet right there on the floor between the couch and the coffee table. There was a long moment of silence even after we were each situated. I could hear him breathing and he was no more asleep then I was.

"Edward?" I rolled on my side and dropped my arm over the edge to find him. My hand came to rest on what I believed to be his shoulder.

"Yes, Green?"

"I think Lily likes you."

Again, more silence which was only broken by a long exhale on Edward's part. I waited, but he said nothing.

"I mean she really likes you."

A muscle tensed and released beneath my hand, not a twitch, just a flex beyond what had been the movement of his skin rising and falling with every breath. Finally his words came through what I heard to be a clinched jaw. "Yes, I figured as much."

There was more silence only broken by the rattling and gurgling of the window unit kicking on.

"And?" I squeaked out above the noise. I wanted to know what he thought of that.

Before I could ask anything else that would expound upon the subject, Edward changed the subject. "My sister, Anne, worked down here for half the summer year before last. Isabella's four years older than I am and Anne's a year younger than I am so she was about your age at the time. She worked with the horses same as me. Mr. Watson and Lily were her host family. Instead of living in the apartment like me, she lived with them. Anne and Lily became good friends."

"So they've kind of been your host family too?"

Edward placed his hand over mine. "Lily and Anne still write to one another. They have some plans to be real sisters and what better way? It's never been in the cards though."

"So you're not interested?" If there was any denying my age, there wasn't now. Older girls would not have asked such a stupid question and as soon as the words left my mouth I regretted it.

Edward snickered and gripped my hand tighter to him. "Go to sleep, Green."

"Lucile Marie Meeks!" I awoke to the startled voice of my mother. It came from down the hall where she had undoubtedly found my bed empty.

There was nothing what-so-ever going on, but both Edward and I scrambled. I wrapped my bed spread around me and ran to the kitchen as light footed as I could.

"I'm in the kitchen!" I yelled back to her.

"Ms. Meeks, is everything alright?" Edward added to the plan to throw her off the trail. I'm sure he knew as well as I did that if she caught us in the living room together, me having slept in there, regardless of me being on the couch and him on the floor, she wouldn't have seen it as the innocent thing it was.

I could hardly breathe before Mama was wrapped all around me. "What did I tell you about scaring me?" Her heart was racing.

"I'm fine. Do we have any bacon?" I wormed my way out of her arms.

A hand across her heart and one on her hip, Mama thought about the question and tried to regain her composure. "Bacon? Let me think."

"I thought we could make breakfast for Edward since he stayed over to protect us."

"There's no need really. A piece of toast if you've got it, but please don't go to any trouble." Edward was busily folding the makings of his pallet.

Again, Mama was scared half out of her wits. Unlike me in my off brand Umbros and a t-shirt, Mama had on little more than a thin nightgown in front of him, a virtual stranger to him. Thank heavens she hadn't opened the living room curtains yet or the morning sun would have shown right through that night gown of hers. And, she didn't have on a shred of make-up. I was certain my mother hadn't been seen by the opposite sex without make-up since she was twelve.

"Excuse me!" Mama shrieked and made for her bedroom.

"Found the bacon!" I grabbed it and the eggs.

Over scrambling eggs and sizzling bacon, Edward was the first person to tell me

"Happy Birthday" that morning. He had excused himself to borrow our bathroom and when he returned that was the first thing he said to me.

"Thanks!" My insides danced.

The first thing I had seen that morning when I woke up was him. His eyes popped open with a smile and they were the promise of a new day. Now his hair was damp and he'd made some effort to style it. He hadn't had the time, but he looked fresh out of the shower. I could have gone on looking at him.

Nothing was said of my night of the couch or our conversation about Lily and nothing was said over breakfast about Dwayne Richards either. It was a new day and maybe we could get past all of the nonsense that was yesterday.

Chapter 9

My memory is not the best. I cannot remember every detail of my birthday party. The faces of most of my guests are a blur. There were only a couple of things that stood out from that night.

What I did remember was the very moment Edward showed up. I remembered the music that was playing and, as usual, Kevin was doing his best to cling to me.

"Lucy, come on!" Kevin reached for my hand to pull me back to our makeshift dance floor in the middle of the living room in the Halfway House. "I know you like this song."

I shirked his grasp and turned to walk away. That's when I noticed Edward standing in the threshold of the front door. It was pitch black outside and it was still falling a downpour. I could only see his outline really, but I knew it was him.

I bit my lip before I could smile too big and Edward stepped into the light. He was drenched.

"I would have been here sooner, but I had to put the top and doors on the Bronco."

Edward shook a little like the hounds did when they were wet and then he ran a hand through his hair. He'd never looked better. I could feel my cheeks flush as the candlelight flickered in his eyes.

"Better late than never," I replied.

Maggie came bouncing over and Lily was only a second behind.

"I'm so glad you came!" Lily cut between Maggie and I and threw her arms around Edward.

Over Lily's shoulder, Edward gave me a once over while Maggie gave me a stern look.

There was something about Lily that Maggie never liked. I always thought Maggie was just being jealous. Maggie could be territorial. I just always figured I was her territory and she didn't like Lily trespassing on me.

"Lily, aren't you going to introduce your friend?" Maggie turned her attention back to the couple before her. Lily didn't notice the tone in Maggie's voice, but I did.

Lily didn't even acknowledge Maggie. "So nice to see a friendly face," Lily fawned over Edward. "I hardly know a soul, but now that you're here I'll have someone to talk to."

Edward slipped free of Lily much like he had done Whitney Knox the first time I'd met him. "Lily, you've had me all to yourself all summer. Surely you've grown tired of me."

"Oh, I could never get tired of you." Lily gave him a pawing pat on his chest and again Maggie glared at me.

Edward tensed as she touched him. Clearly Lily was behaving a little more familiar than Edward liked. He stepped to the side to give some distance.

"Happy birthday, Green."

My stomach did a flip and I was afraid I couldn't squeak out a word, but I managed.

"Hi." I tilted my head, "This is Maggie, my best friend."

Lily closed the gap Edward had put between them. She clung to him, still staking her claim.

Edward extended his hand. "Nice to meet you Maggie."

I was about to introduce him, but Lily did the honors. "This is Edward."

"Edward's been teaching me to ride," I added.

"And have you been a good student?" Maggie teased.

"The best," Edward added.

I blushed and Lily sulked. I'm sure she was starting to regret loaning me her horse.

"Edward," Lily drooled, "Would you mind dancing with me before Lucy has to cut her cake?"

Edward looked me straight in the eyes and exhaled. "Sure, Lily."

"Let's get something to drink, Maggie." I took Maggie one way while Lily pulled Edward another.

I tried to keep in mind that it was only by the grace of God that Lily was still with us and I had never suffered like she had so begrudging her a dance with the guy of both of our dreams would be awful selfish of me. I didn't want to be that kind of person.

"He's cute!"

"Way to state the obvious, Maggie," I laughed as we headed toward the dining room.

Mama and Mr. Watson were manning the punch bowl and snacks.

"Are you having a good time, Lucy?"

"Yes, sir," I answered as Mr. Watson handed me a cup of Mama's famous lime sherbet punch.

"Looks like Lily's having a good time too," Mama called our attention to Lily and Edward dancing.

It was kind of funny. The song was Kokomo by the Beach Boys. Aside of Lily looking like a little girl dancing with a grown man, they were slow dancing and everyone else who was left on the floor was fast dancing.

I dared not laugh in front of Mr. Watson. I felt sorry for him and Lily. I furrowed my brow and Maggie shook her head.

"Thanks for the punch."

Maggie and I returned to the living room and mingled with others that were not occupied by dancing. All the while I think Maggie watched Lily and Edward as much as I did. At the turn of the song, Maggie cut in and scooped Edward from Lily's clutches. I tried not to revel in the look on Lily's face, again reminding myself that I didn't want to be that person. I didn't want to be the person that took pleasure in Lily's suffering.

I chatted with Kevin and Thomas and a few of the girls from my softball team. I tried to focus on the conversations at hand. Everyone assumed I did well on my driver's test this morning so the natural question was what kind of car I was going to get and when I was going to get it.

"I hope I'll be able to buy one by the end of summer. I've been saving everything I've made at the kennel so far and my grandmother said she would match whatever I had when school starts back."

"Let me know how much Nanny gives you because she always gives me the exact thing she gives you." Thomas could hardly contain his excitement. Thomas was seven months younger than me.

"I don't know how much she'll give you." I repeated myself and explained to him what she meant about matching me.

"What?" His excitement faded like a popped balloon.

"Well, if she just gave you the money then she would be buying it for you. The point is for you to work for it yourself." Kevin took up where I left off with the explanation.

Thomas rolled his eyes. He wasn't a fan of work. He was sort of the family joke even his mother knew it.

"Thomas wasn't afraid of work," his mother, Aunt Joyce, would say. "He'll sit right next to it all day long."

I tried not to watch Edward and Maggie as I answered the question as to what kind of car I wanted.

"I would really like a Rabbit, a convertible one. Remember those?" That was my practical choice.

"Seriously?" Lily interjected. I had forgotten that she was lingering around the outskirts of the group. "You want the Barbie car you had when you were ten?"

The entire group laughed.

Maggie and Edward's song ended and Maggie rejoined the group. "What she really wants is a cherry red Alpha Romeo Spider, but since her mother works for the cheapest attorney in town..."

"Maggie stop it."

I didn't want Maggie to be the person that got at Lily either. I knew it wasn't exactly fair, but Lily could take all the shots at me she wanted. If Maggie or I took any shots back, we'd be the bad guys.

"Time to cut the cake," my mother announced and just in time.

We cut the cake. We opened presents and the music kept playing. It wasn't like the parties when I was little where Mama shooed everyone out the door as soon as I had ripped open all of the pretty wrapping paper. She had given me until midnight before she said she would shut this one down.

If the clock above the mantle in the Halfway House was correct, it was just about ten and putting what I thought was the last present to the side when Mr. Watson handed me another.

"This is from me and Lily."

Lily had been seated on one side of me and Maggie was on the other.

"I can't wait to see what it is. He picked it out himself and refused to tell me what it was," Lily explained.

It was a small box, with red paper.

"I'm sorry. When I went looking for wrapping paper this afternoon, all I could find in the house was the Christmas leftovers."

"It's fine," I assured him as I started to tear it open.

Inside the little box was a photo. It was an old Polaroid that was turning black, but I could make out who was in it. It was Mr. Watson when he appeared to be about my age and he was standing in front of an old Mustang. Under the photo was a set of keys.

Puzzlement was written all over my face and Mr. Watson stepped closer to explain. "It was my first car and I figured..."

"What?" Lily gasped. "You gave her a car?"

Mr. Watson tried to keep his composure, but he didn't like it when Lily spoke against him. No parent that I knew did like those kind of out bursts from their children, especially in public.

"You said you didn't want it," he politely reminded her.

"But..."

"I can't take it. It's too much." I put the photo back in the box and handed it to Lily.

Lily hardly had it in her hand when Mr. Watson took it from her and handed it back to me. "No. I want you to have it and that's the end of it. It's in great shape and it's just sitting in the barn."

I couldn't believe Mama didn't say anything other than, "Lucy, say thank you."

I didn't want to make a scene in front of all of my friends. I didn't want to be the fool that turned down a free car. What sort of person did that?

"Thank you?" It came out more like a question than a statement and there was certainly no excitement in it.

Lily stormed out of the room and Mr. Watson followed. While they were in the other room Edward seized the opportunity to ask me to dance.

It wasn't Pearl Jam, but it was the same Rock Alt that played when I danced with Edward. "Lightening Crashes" by Live. It stared out slow, but then picked up speed. Dancing with him, I suspected I might not have been the only one who took dance lessons, but that was a silly thought. Unlike dancing with Kevin, Edward led and he kept perfect time with the music and to the beat. When he spun me toward the end of the song it took my breath more than when he held me close.

When Edward spun me back into his arms he whispered in my ear, "After the song ends wait two songs and then excuse yourself to the bathroom. There's a door next to the bathroom that's another staircase. The stairs lead to the basement. I'm going say my good-byes and make my excuses to leave right after this song. I'll meet you down there and give you my present then."

I nodded in agreement. "Okay." I wondered what it could be that he wanted to give it to me in private. Just one dance with him was enough of a present for me.

After the last note, Edward thanked me for the dance, told me "happy birthday" again and then made his way to Mr. Watson. From Mr. Watson he went to Lily and told her he was leaving. She begged him to stay, but he gave her the excuse that the hunt was going out early the next morning so he needed to get to bed.

Edward also said good-bye to Maggie and a few other of my friends with whom she was holding court.

"It was great to meet you," he told her. He gave her the same excuse he had given Lily for having to leave early. Maggie didn't press Edward the way Lily had.

Lily saw him to the door and I acted nonchalant about it, but it was as devastating for me to see him go as it was for Lily. The difference between Lily and I is that I was certain I would see him again in a few minutes.

Those few minutes seemed like an eternity, but the second song finally ended and I did as he asked. I found the staircase just where he said it would be. Luckily there was a light on at the bottom or I would have been terrified to go down there by myself.

I didn't find Edward waiting in the basement, but I found the door to the outside open. "Edward," I whispered out the door.

The Halfway House was built on brick pillars that lifted the house about ten feet off of the ground as if it was on stilts. The basement was enclosed sometime far after the time it was initially built. The pillars were spaced along the underside support to the main part of the house. The main floor over hung the pillars and the basement was built within them. One of the pillars was right beside the door.

There was no verbal response to me saying his name. Instead, Edward stepped to the doorway and offered me his hand. I could feel the smile rising on my face as I accepted his offer and felt his touch. His hands were so soft that I feared they were softer than mine.

The rain had slacked off a little and it wasn't coming down in sheets so I had no hesitation in following him as he pulled me outside. The floor above over hung the support by about three feet so there was no real danger of me getting wet and having some explaining to go when I returned.

Every move with him was an adventure in anticipation. What was he going to give me?

Under the house we crept and finally turned around to me. We stopped right by one of the pillars.

"You know I'm too old for you, right?" Edward asked as he ran his finger tips from my neck across my bare shoulder.

Chill bumps went rushing down my legs and there was a burning sensation in the pit of my stomach. I nodded, giving only a slight indication of my agreement.

"You've got two more years of high school and..." he paused and stepped closer to me.

It was 10:00 p.m. and the only thing that gave light to his face was a street light that was rigged up in the back yard of the house. We were in the shadows, but my eyes were locked in his and I could see him as plain as ever.

His hand that ran over my shoulder continued down my arm until it found my hand at my side. Edward slipped that hand in mine and locked our fingers. His other hand went behind my neck and into my hair.

"I can't sneak around with you and that's what we would have to do for Lily's sake."

"I know." The words escaped with the rise and fall of my chest and he came closer and backed me into the pillar.

"Your mother wouldn't approve if she knew." He pressed his nose to my forehead.

As if I had no other words, I exhaled again, "I know," and I stood on my toes to lift my face closer to his.

From my neck he moved his hand to my chin and the other that was holding my hand found my waist. "You are so beautiful."

No boy had ever told me I was beautiful before.

His voice was lower. "I want to kiss you anyway." I could feel his words against my cheeks.

Flips. That's what my stomach was doing and, my knees, they were going weak. I wanted him to kiss me. I wanted it desperately.

"Do it," I breathed.

There was a moment of just him breathing as if he was working up the courage or trying to fight off the urge, I'm not sure which. Then as my heart pounded and I ran my fingers through the hair on the back of his head, he did it.

It was soft and short and he backed away, took a quick look at me and came back for a second. Was it really a second or just the continuation of the first? I could hardly breathe. Edward's kiss was what a first kiss should be, soft and gentle and the definition of passion. At the same time it brought a wave of peacefulness over me like I had never known. It was the kind of kiss that I would never forget and never get over.

I told myself that time and time again. I wanted Edward for myself, but I didn't want Lily to be hurt. I knew the best thing to do would be to put him out of my mind, but kissing him was my version of heaven on earth.

That kiss under the overhang with the rain still dripping was what made the Halfway House the perfect place to have my birthday party and the one thing from the evening that I would remember most.

Chapter 10

Of course the kiss felt like it could go on forever, but not even the best kisses, the ones that fairy tales were built around could do that. It had to end and it did.

The sound of footsteps coming down the basement stairs was hardly a distraction, but the sound of Mr. Watson's voice was. It gave us pause, but we didn't move a muscle. The basement door was still open and Edward and I were both terrified of being discovered. All anyone had to do was stick their head out the door and they would have spotted us.

"Why are we down here?" he asked.

"Because this isn't a conversation to have upstairs where anyone might hear us." My mother's was the first set of shoes we heard on the stairs.

"What conversation?"

"Boyd, you've got to stop." Her voice was adamant.

"Stop what?"

Edward and I waited, both knowing we shouldn't be hearing them. Edward shifted slightly so his back was to the door and she shielded me from the sight of it.

"Stop giving Lucy things especially things that are inappropriate, too grand."

"Why?" Mr. Watson was as adamant in his question as Mama was with her warning.

"She doesn't appreciate it." Mama continued.

"What teenager doesn't appreciate a free car? How ungrateful can she be?"

"Lucy is her own person. She wants to make her own choices even if she has to work for what she wants. She sees you as taking away her choices and making decisions for her that you have no right to make. She resents you for it."

On one side of us was the open door. On the other side of us was a window. I couldn't see in the window, but when I looked away from Edward, I could see their shadows shining through. Mainly, I could see his and he was pacing.

I wanted so badly to cheer for Mama, to add my two cents to the conversation

I was almost desperate for it. Edward could tell. He widened his eyes to make sure my attention was back with him.

"I have every..."

"No, you don't. Didn't you see Lily's face just now? She was heartbroken. You gave your first car to someone other than her, your only child. You don't think she might have wanted that car?"

There was a loud huff from Mr. Watson, so loud we could hear it through the doorway. I could just imagine him slapping his head in exasperation.

"Lily can't even drive."

"You know Lucy failed her driver's test this morning?"

"You think you're some father to her, but you're not. You don't know her, not really. You certainly don't know her the way a father should and you're dangerously close to not knowing Lily either."

"Of course I know Lily!"

"Do you? Then you know she's mad for that boy that you practically have living with you."

My breath caught in my throat and I studied Edward's face. We touched on the subject last night, but he shut it down.

"Somehow we've got to get you back inside." I could hardly hear him, but I could feel his breath on my ear. It sent chills down my legs again.

I nodded still listening to Mama and Mr. Watson and both of us still not wanting to be caught. I just wanted them to go back upstairs and leave me to kiss Edward again. As far as I was concerned, their nonsense could wait one more day.

"Lily thinks of him like a brother."

"Are you kidding me? Boyd Watson you are a fool!"

"Mary Meeks!"

"You are! You are a fool if you don't see Lily throwing herself at that boy. Honestly and right under your nose. You're a fool and she's making a fool of herself."

"She's just a baby!" Mr. Watson might as well have stated that he was ignorant.

"Lily's five years older than Lucy and you just gave Lucy a car. Perspective, Boyd. Come on!"

Another Watson huff.

"She's throwing herself at him and you mean to tell me you haven't even noticed and what's worse is she's starting to see Lucy as competition. Is that what you want? The one true friend Lily has and she's about to alienate her and because of you. Because you don't see what's right in front of your nose. She's frail. She's been sick all her life, but she's not a baby. She's a young lady. A young lady that's long overdue to take an interest in boys. Lord, Lucy's been boy crazy for three years now and I've had my work cut out for me. What have you done, Boyd? You've let the fox in the hen house."

I think both Edward and I resisted the urge to gasp. My resistance was for being called boy crazy and Edward having heard that. Edward's resistance was for being called the fox in the hen house. I think we were both as embarrassed as the other.

Finally Mama stormed back upstairs. Her voice faded as she went up. "I've got to go make sure none of them are burning the place down."

Mr. Watson belted out, "Mary! God dammit!" I could just imagine him rolling his eyes and shaking his head. Mr. Watson lingered for a moment and then headed up the stairs.

As soon as he was certain they were gone, Edward backed away from me. My heart

156

immediately sank. He let go of my hands and my heart nearly stopped altogether.

"I'm sorry, Green."

"Sorry for what?"

"This can't go anywhere. I shouldn't have..." He looked down and let out a long exaggerated breath. "I just..."

"I've got to get back inside. Thanks for coming." I smiled and turned to go in.

I wasn't "boy crazy" as Mama had put it. I was just crazy over one boy, one specific boy ... him. As far as I was concerned this night was perfect and if he kept talking he was only going to ruin it. So I stopped him. I went back upstairs and devoted the rest of the night to Lily and Maggie and the rest of my friends.

The next day I slept until almost noon. I dreamed of Edward. Kiss after kiss, he was mine. When I woke up I knew he was right. It couldn't go anywhere. There was only a three year age gap but college boys worth having didn't date high school girls. He was worth having and he was smart and he could have any girl he wanted so what was in it for him to date a high school girl. Was it a summer fling? I didn't think so. There was a thought churning around in my brain that told me he was the love of my life. Even I knew that was a silly notion.

Mr. Watson pulled in with the Mustang around 1:00 p.m. It was as cherry red and a fastback. It looked just like the one in the photo he had given me. It was still weird for him to include the photo, but I never could figure him out.

Edward rode with him in his car so he could carry him back. Lily wasn't with them and that was strange. They didn't stay. They dropped off the car and left. Edward only made eye contact with me once. I think Mr. Watson might have been taking stock of some of what Mama said to him last night in the basement and I think Edward and I were done before we ever really started. My birthday present from him had been that I had a boyfriend for my sixteenth birthday, but only for that one night and it was a secret boyfriend at that.

"I guess you can take your driver's test again in this thing come Monday." Mama slid her hand down the side of the car, admiring it.

"Maybe."

"What happened with that anyway? I know your grandmother's been letting you drive for years so..."

"You know about that?"

"Of course. There's nothing you can do that people around town don't tell me. Don't you know that by now, Lucy?"

Thanks to Dwayne, knowing that Mama was somehow watching me was kind of a comforting thought now.

I thought about the Mustang all day and all night. It was a bit of a break from thinking of Edward. It really was a beautiful car, I thought as I admired it through the window from my spot on the living room couch. It was beautiful and it galled me that I wanted to keep it. I was full of pride and a little bit of spite, but I wasn't stupid. As Mr. Watson said, "What teenager doesn't want a free car?"

I finally decided that my best course of action was to pay him for the Mustang. On the way to my driving test Monday morning, I had Nanny stop by Wally's and I picked up a copy of an Auto Trader magazine. I found an ad in there for the closest match to Mr. Watson's Mustang. Seven thousand dollars is what the ad said they wanted for the car. I just about choked on my gum. None-the-less, I would offer him seven thousand and pay him two hundred dollars per month until I had it paid off. I didn't know how I was going to get the money considering I wasn't real sure I still had a job at the kennel, but I would figure out something.

Plus, if I was buying the car, maybe this would take the edge off of Lily. She made it obvious at my party that she didn't like that he had given it to me. I didn't blame her. If Mama had something so valuable, and clearly sentimental, and she passed me over and gave it to someone else, I would have been hurt and irritated. As Nanny would say, "That would have chapped my ass!"

After my driving test, which I passed this time, I asked Nanny to take me by Mr. Watson's office. She occupied Mama while I asked for a moment of Mr.

Watson's time. I was fortunate that he didn't have any clients waiting and I was able to go straight back.

"Well what brings you in this morning and what can I do for you, Lucy?" Mr. Watson offered me one of the chairs across from his desk before he took a seat.

"I know what Mama said about me just saying 'Thank you' for the car, but I just don't feel right about accepting it. I was telling the truth on so many levels.

"So you want to give it back?" He adjusted his reading glasses and turned his attention to sorting the files on his desk.

"Not exactly." I flipped the pages and held out the Auto Trader. I pointed to the specific ad. "I figured since this one is going for seven thousand and it's basically the same, then I'll pay you that for yours."

"You have seven thousand dollars?" He looked over his glasses and square at me. I'm sure he already knew the answer.

"Well, no, but..." I reached in my pocket pulled out the money I'd just drained my savings account to get. I proceeded to explain to him my payment plan. "Here's four hundred now, this month's and next. Next month I'll go ahead and give you payment so I'll always stay ahead by a month."

"Staying ahead is a good plan, but Lucy, honestly, it was a gift and I wanted you to have it." Mr. Watson scratched his head and contemplated his next statement. "Look, if this arrangement will make you feel better, then it's fine."

"It will. Thank you." I reached out my hand and we shook on it.

"By the way, any word on Dwayne?" I asked.

"You don't need to concern yourself with him," Mr. Watson answered. The subject to of Dwayne Richards was still as sore for him as it was for me.

"I kind of have to. You see, I just bought a car so I kind of need that job at the kennel." I smiled and shrugged my shoulders.

If Mr. Watson laughed like that and made the effort to understand me like he did just then, I might stop looking for reasons to despise him. Maybe the talk Mama gave him on Saturday night really was sinking in.

"If you still want the job it's yours, plus we've just had an opening for a supervisory position that pays a little more money. I mean, since you just bought a car, more money might be nice."

I couldn't have been happier. "Thank you so much!"

I ran around his desk and hugged him. That's the first time I could ever remember hugging Mr. Watson. I was in a state of shock over it myself and I quickly let go. When I stepped back, he looked like he had tears in his eyes. Strange, but whatever. I had to get to work.

I grabbed Nanny and rushed home. No sooner had she dropped me off than did I turn the key in the ignition for the Mustang. One turn and it fired right up. I tapped the gas and it made a "Wommppp, wommmpp, wommmpp" sound. Heads turned all the way through Thomson. I had always liked driving, but now I loved driving. This was the stuff car commercials were made of.

"Honey-child, I didn't think you'd be back here after Friday." Mrs. Pope dropped the water hose. The handle of the nozzle hit the concrete and sprayed us both. She gave it a little kick to tip it over.

A little shower didn't stop Mrs. Pope from throwing both arms around me and squeezing tight. She was glad to see me. With Dwayne in the wind, she had been there all by herself until I got there. The kennel wasn't a ton of work on a daily basis, but it was more than enough for one person just with feeding and hosing the stalls let alone training and running the hounds.

"Well, here I'm. I need the job." I laughed at my circumstances.

"I know how that goes."

She gave me an empathetic pat on the back and we got to work.

Monday afternoon at the kennel was peaceful, a nice change. Tuesday was even better except there was no riding lesson. Both days I found myself gazing in the direction of the hunt barn every chance I got. I wondered what Edward was doing and if he

162

thought of me. Was he somewhere looking at the kennel wondering what I was doing?

Wednesday came and I hadn't seen or heard from Edward since he dropped off the Mustang with Mr. Watson on Sunday. I put my jeans and riding boots in the car yesterday morning just in case, but nothing. I wondered if I would be invited out with the hunt again today or if maybe my lessons had been moved and they forgot to tell me.

I continued about my morning and finally Mrs. Pope stuck her head out of the office and yelled for me. "Lucy, Edward's on the phone. He wants you to come up for your lesson."

I finished throwing out the bucket of chicken to the hounds in the stall I was in before going to wash up. I headed for the barn and grabbed my clothes along the way, changed in the bathroom at the hunt barn and on to Blueberry's stall.

As usual I helped with the saddle for Blueberry. The stall was more cramped than it normally was. There was a thickness in the air which was made more conspicuous with Edward and me continually brushing into one another. The horse jerked when the saddle went over and nearly crushed me between one of his hind legs and the wall. Edward snatched me out of the way and into him.

"Be careful where you step!" Edward snapped.

"Sorry."

A few more run-ins and Edward threw up his hands. "I can't do this! Finish him yourself and meet me in the front pasture." Edward stormed out, leaving me confused. I wasn't sure what it was he couldn't handle, but I followed his orders and finished the saddle myself.

The lesson was bitter, more barking and frustration from Edward. Time wasn't quite up, but I'd had enough.

I hopped off of Blueberry in the middle of the pasture. "I don't know what your problem is, but if you are trying to be an ass, you're making out in spades!"

I took Blueberry by the lead and headed back to the stable on foot. Out of the corner of my eye I saw someone leaning on the fence watching. It was Lily and Molly's car was pulling out onto the road.

Lily met me at the stall. I went about taking the saddle down. It was some work, heavier than I thought and it nearly came crashing down on my head. Lily tried to help me and it took the both of us just to sit it in the corner of the stall.

"You know, if lessons are too hard, you can quit." Lily heard what transpired between Edward and I in the pasture.

"I'm not a quitter." I reached for the brushes in the tack bucket, one for me and one for Lily.

"But I don't know how." She tried to keep from taking the brush.

"Then it's high time you learned. After all, he's your horse."

"Fine."

While Lily helped me brush down Blueberry I seized the opportunity. "Do you know how to drive?"

"No."

"Wanna learn?"

"What?"

"I'll teach you."

"You just got your license two days ago."

"I know, but I've been driving since I was eight years old."

Lily was about to say something else, but I cut her off. "Yes or no, Lily."

Lily took her time and kept brushing. Finally she answered, "Okay."

"We'll start tomorrow after I get off work."

We kept brushing and when we were finished Lily asked me if I was going out with the hunt that afternoon.

"I don't think so. I haven't been asked. Plus, with Dwayne gone, I have to make sure the hounds are ready and then get put up afterward." I turned and put the brushes away.

"You can ride with me and Mrs. Pope so you don't have to wait around here by yourself."

"I supposed."

We didn't lose any hounds that night and they didn't get on the scent of a coyote or a fox. The most memorable thing was that I overheard some talk about Dwayne.

"According to his Mama, he's gone to her brother's house in North Carolina," Mrs. Harper told Mrs. Hobbs.

"I think he should be locked up," Mrs. Hobbs responded. "I mean, after what he did to the girl two summers ago and now this."

"Bobby says they're gonna let him be as long as he doesn't come back to Georgia."

Bobby was Mr. Harper's first name and he used to be with the sheriff's department. I didn't know all of the members outside of the club, but I knew the Harpers. Mr. Harper had been good friends with my dad.

That night at home I asked Mama what she knew about it.

"Well, Lucy, as it turned out, he didn't really flee after leaving you in the woods. He went home and grabbed the things that he'd already packed for a weekend of fishing with his uncle."

"Oh, so he thought he would just go on like nothing had happened?"

"I think so. When the deputies went back to serve the warrant at his mother's, she told 'em she didn't know anything about him running off and that the fishing trip had been planned since before he graduated."

I shook my head.

Mama passed me the plates to set the table for dinner. "His mama's pretty upset about it."

"I imagine." The only thing I was upset about was that he was just going to get off.

"What's wrong? He's not going to bother you anymore. For all intents and purposes, he's essentially banished from McDuffie County so he won't be coming back here."

"He just gets away with it?"

"No, Lucy. He doesn't get to come home. That's not getting away with it."

I sat the plates down. "He doesn't even have to..."

"What do you want, Lucy?" She had put half of the spaghetti noodles in the pot and Mama just stood there with the rest of them in her hand.

"I want...God...I want him to know what he did was wrong! I want to see his face and know that he knows and know that he can't do anything else to me or anyone else!"

"What do you mean anyone else?" Mama cocked an eye at me.

"I overheard Mrs. Hobbs say something about a girl last year. That he did something to a girl last year."

"I don't know anything about that, Lucy, but what I do know is that you need to let it go."

I sulked all through dinner. I wondered about the other girl and then it finally hit me. Edward's sister, he said she was here two summers ago.

I finished dinner and then told Mama I couldn't remember if I locked the door at the kennel. I didn't go to the kennel. I went straight to the Watson's.

Chapter 11

I marched to the door and whaled on the door bell, hitting it multiple times. Honestly the bell hardly made it through the first three notes of "Dixie" before I hit it again. If Mr. Watson knew whatever it was Dwayne had done to Edward's sister and he sent me to work at the kennel with that boy anyway, I was going to kick him.

Mr. Watson snatched the door open and my being there caught him totally off guard. "Lucy, what's the matter?"

"Did you know?!!" Still on the front porch, I tried to refrain from screaming in his face and bringing out all of the neighbors.

"Did I know what?"

As his face drained of all of its color, I saw Lily over his shoulder. She was coming down the stairs. Noticing my distraction, Mr. Watson checked behind him. He saw Lily there, doe-eyed and curious as to what the issue was.

"Lucy is having a problem with the car. We're going to take it for a drive and see if I can tell what it is. I don't know how long it'll take so don't wait up on me," Mr. Watson told Lily.

When he turned around I was almost in his face. "Lying is just so easy for you!" It was more than a whisper, but not loud enough that Lily would hear.

"Keys please." Mr. Watson held out his hand.

I rolled my eyes and slammed the keys into his hand.

We took a right out of the driveway and headed down Lee Street in silence. We were on the Washington Highway before I asked him again. "Did you know?"

I watched for any change in his expression, any signal that would give him away. I knew him to be a liar, but I could never tell when he was doing it.

"You know, I'm not the awful person you think I am. I've never wanted anything, but the best for you."

"I'm going to ask you again. Did you know?" I gritted my teeth. He knew and he was trying to squirm out of telling me.

"Yes! I knew. I've known all along." Mr. Watson didn't bother with the blinker and made the turn at the church and headed toward Lincolnton.

"How could you? You just said you wanted the best for me, but you sent me to work out there..."

"Wait, hold on, what are we talking about?" Mr. Watson absentmindedly took his foot off the gas and the car started to slow. He took his eyes off of the road and turned his full attention to me.

"Dwayne and the kennel and how he did something to Edward's sister. Like you don't know!"

"What?!!" He grabbed his breath, completely taken aback. "No! What are you talking about?"

I twisted in my seat to face him and braced myself with a hand on the dash. "What are *you* talking about?"

Mr. Watson put his foot back on the gas and ran a hand through his hair. "Jesus Christ, Lucy. I swore to your mother I wouldn't be the one to tell you." He shook his head.

"If it isn't about Dwayne, what exactly is it that you've known about all along? And don't you lie to me!" I pressed him.

Mr. Watson let out a long breath and drew in an equally long one. "Let's just get something straight. Short of the lie I just told Lily, I've told one lie in my entire life. One. It's a doozy, but I'm not the habitual liar you seem to think I am!"

"Whatever."

"If we're going to have a serious conversation, lose the attitude."

"You're not my father."

"Well, are you proud of yourself? You've been dying to say that for years? Do you feel better now?"

"Yeah!"

Mr. Watson pulled off of the side of the road and started checking the road behind.

"What are you doing?" I asked him as I looked behind as well.

"Making a U-turn."

"Why?"

"I'm taking you home."

"Huh?"

"You don't seem willing to have a civil conversation so I might as well take you home."

"Wait!" I ordered him and was immediately disgusted with myself. I didn't like him any better, but he had a point. I was acting like a child.

"Are you going to listen and stop being so judgmental?"

Begrudgingly, I turned on a respectful tone, "Yes, sir."

Mr. Watson eased back onto the road and we continued across the bridge over Clarks Hill at Raysville Marina.

"Lucy, have you ever done something that you should regret, but you didn't?"

I thought about my situation with Lily and Edward. I should have regretted getting mixed up with him, knowing how Lily felt about him, but all I thought about was kissing him. I should have regretted the kiss, but I didn't. I wanted to do it again.

I didn't deny that I knew what Mr. Watson was talking about. "Yes, sir."

"I did something once that I should have regretted, but I don't. I feel bad about how it has affected others, but I don't regret it. That probably makes me a bad person, but I've spent a lifetime trying to make up for it. I've spent your lifetime trying to make up for it."

"I don't understand."

"Shall I start from the beginning?"

"Please."

"When I was a little older than you are now, I fell in love for the first time. To be completely honest, it was the only time. I remember the first time I ever laid eyes on her. It was at the homecoming football game. Thomson was playing Aquinas and she was in the homecoming court. She won that night. How clichéd, right? I fell in love with the homecoming queen, but who wouldn't? You've seen photos of your mother. She was the dream of every boy in the CSRA that had ever laid eyes on her. I will spare you the details since she's your mother."

I blushed at his description of her.

Mr. Watson kept driving as he went on with the story. "I didn't go to school at Thomson and I was only at the game on the invitation of my cousin, Michael. He went to school there. I went to Augusta Christian. Even though your mother had a date, you know him, Bobby Harper, I asked her to dance. To this day, I remember exactly what I said to her."

Mr. Watson paused for a moment and shook his head. He was clearly reliving the memory.

"What did you say?" I was curious.

He let out a slight chuckle. "I told her, 'When I was eight I wanted a bicycle and I got one. When I was sixteen I wanted a car and I got one. I'm eighteen and I want you."

"Oh." All I could think was that he hadn't changed a bit. Still full of himself.

"I got her. We dated all of about six months until my mother put an end to it."

"Why?"

"My mother was a very, very religious woman and if you didn't go to *the* Baptist Church, you were not worthy. Back then, your mother went to the Church of God, which my mother equated with...Let's just say it might as well have been a cult as far as she was concerned."

"Your mother was heartbroken and I wasn't any better. My mother saw the way I looked at her and it didn't matter. 'No son of mine's wasting his life and squandering the family name.' That's what she said. 'You'll break if off with her or I will.'"

After the bridge Mr. Watson made a turn into Amity Park, weaved around through the woods and found a place to park. He got out and came around. I was opening my door when he caught hold of the outside handle.

"Come with me." He held out his hand to help me.

"I got it. Thanks."

Mr. Watson continued with what he had to say when we found an empty swing out by the point.

"I like sitting out here watching the boats go by. Every time Lily takes a turn I find myself right back out here, staring into the water and begging the Lord for a little more time with her."

"After all this time I don't blame my mother for what happened between me and Mary. One day, when you have children of your own, you'll understand. You will do anything to protect them, to give them the best start in life you can. You'll do whatever it takes to keep them on the path you put them on. Can't say I'd do much different than she did. In fact, I've done worse."

"What exactly did she do and what have you done?"

"She put her foot down. She let me know in no uncertain terms that she held the purse strings and what my options were: marry your mother and kiss college good-bye, kiss my family good-bye as we'd never be welcome again or, well, you know the alternative already."

"What sort of life would we have had? No money. No education beyond high school. No family."

"I told my mother I'd join the army and make my own family. She promptly reminded me that I broke my leg in three places when I was a child and the military didn't take soldier with steel rods in their legs."

Mr. Watson patted his left thigh. "It makes a good weather vane, but it's no good for marching through the jungle or anywhere else."

"I don't remember your mother being that awful."

"You wouldn't. She was kind to most everyone's face. And, beyond the religion issue, she didn't really have a problem with your mother, but that was a big one.  More importantly, my mother wanted me to make something of myself and if I had married anyone straight out of high school the likelihood of that happening was slim and none."

"I really don't see where this is going."  I was getting impatient.  Plus, the sun was starting to set and knew my mother would be worried if I didn't get home soon and I was still just damn mad with him.

"Give me a minute.  I'm getting there."

Mr. Watson gave the ground a push with his foot to get the swing going again and he went on.  "The short version is I gave your mother some excuse as to why it could go nowhere.  I was pretty convincing, but didn't breathe a word about my mother being the culprit.  If I had she'd never have let me go."

"You say that as if she's ever let you go."  I looked straight through him.

"Just listen. It was bad, a real bad break-up for both of us.  I went off to UGA and she got stuck here.  It's not been easy for her, you know.  She married the very next boy she dated.  I don't mean to sound conceited, but it was a rebound on her part."

I rolled my eyes, but he didn't notice.  "NO!"  My nostrils flared and I huffed.

"I think he loved her…"

"He did love her!"  I snapped.

"He probably did," he agreed.

"What do you know?!"  I never liked anyone saying or implying anything bad about my father.

"I know a great deal more than you," he challenged. "Shall I go on?"

"Fine." I crossed my arms and sat back in the swing.

"You know he was older than she was and a local celebrity of sorts. He was in Vietnam and saved four other guys in his platoon. Think about the couple they made, the homecoming queen and the war hero."

"I moved on too. Your mother had introduced me to her friend, Lila, once and later we ran into one another at college. We had your mother in common. She's the one that told me your mother was married. The news broke my heart all over again and I did my own rebounding. Of course Lily knows nothing about this. She thinks I met her mother at college, but that's it."

I shot another judgmental look at him.

"I know what you're thinking. I didn't lie to her. I just didn't tell her I married her mother while I loved someone else."

I kept listening and he kept explaining.

"I know you've always been a little protective of your father's memory, but I want you to understand that you didn't know him like your mother did. Being in a war does things to people. It scars them and the scars aren't always noticeable at first."

"Just stop!" As far as I was concerned, he wasn't going to tell lies about my father who wasn't there to defend himself.

"Lucy?" He paused after my name.

I gave him a glaring look.

Cautiously, Mr. Watson started again. "Things were fine at first. They made it a year before he disappeared from time to time. He always came back. He lost his job and he lost the next job and he lost the one after that. Your mother thought she was going to be a housewife, but she had to become the breadwinner."

Another glaring look, "That's when she went to work for you?"

"No, first she went to work at Bi-Lo. About a year later, after I finished law school, Lila and I moved back. We had Lily by then and she was already suffering with leukemia. I ran into your mother."

"So you had an affair?" I thought I was stating the obvious.

"That's kind of cutting to the chase."

"Well?"

"It wasn't quite like that. I hadn't seen her in years and there she was, the cashier at BiLo and she was as beautiful as ever. I was haggard. I hadn't slept in days. We moved back to Thomson because our families were here and we could have help taking care of Lily. No sooner had I opened my office than did Lila get sick. I hadn't slept in days. I was busting my ass getting the office off the ground and staying up all night taking care of them or going back and forth to hospitals. I couldn't have her see me like that. The lawyer my mother wanted me to become, a wife from the right church and the right family and I looked like a vagabond. I left my basket of groceries and snuck out of the store, praying she hadn't seen me."

"Jesus, get to the point! I told Mama I was just going to run to the kennel. If I don't get home soon, she's gonna be worried. Could you possibly give me the cliff notes version?"

"Fine! My wife was dying and I had her reach out to your mother. They rekindled their friendship. One thing led to another and at Lila's insistence, your mother and I came to be friends and she came to work for me. Walking in the office and seeing her there was the bright spot of my day. Even when she wasn't there I could still smell her perfume, lavender and jasmine."

"Anyway, she was saddled with a husband that needed something more to live for and I wondered if there was any hope for Lily. I would have done anything for Lily and your mother. I don't know how we came up with it. She figured a baby would be a wake-up call for him. They'd been married for about seven years and they'd been trying for three years with no luck. Her doctor said she was fine so it had to be him. Your mother also mentioned new treatments for leukemia patients, bone marrow transplants and that siblings were usually the best matches. Lila was fading so that wasn't going to happen, I thought. Your mother suggested we solve each other's problems."

My mouth fell open. He didn't need to go on, I was getting the picture.

"No!" I gasped. "No, you're not!"

"I am and I'm so sorry."

Tears filled my eyes. On one hand I couldn't believe it, but on the other it all made perfect sense. That explained so much.

"You're not!"

"Lucy, we had you and you didn't solve anything, but you're the glue that's held all of us together. You're the glue that made me understand why my mother did what she did to me and your mother. I told you. I've done worse to protect my child, but you're my child too."

I covered my mouth with both hands. He reached out to me and I jerked by, refusing to let him touch me.

"They told us there were tests they could do on you to see. We let them. One time, it was awful for you. That scar on your left hip, that's where they took it."

I gasped and snatched back farther from him. My back was pressed more than firmly against the far arm of the swing. I didn't know where the scar came from and it was under my bathing suit line so no one had ever seen it.

"You were so tiny and you cried and cried. It was just ear piercing and heart-wrenching. I refused to let them do anything else to you. I had your well-being to think about as well as Lily's then."

"We found out pretty quickly that you were only a Bandaid for Robert Meeks' problems."

There was no place else to scoot on the swing so to my feet I went. "Don't talk about him!"

It was all I could do just to get air in and let it out. I might as well have been bobbing out there in the lake for all that I was able to breathe. I felt like I had been run over by one of the boats.

"Robert fell in line for a while and he loved you. God, if he ever loved anyone or anything it was you, but he couldn't control himself. You know those boards nailed to the tree across the street from your house?"

"Stop it!" I think he thought I nodded, but really I was just trying to keep my head up straight and stop the swimming feeling. I turned and started back toward the path that led us to the swing. I didn't want to hear anything else.

Mr. Watson chased after me.

"Lucy, you can't possibly remember him. You know that tree across the street from your house with the boards nailed up it? We always said it was what was left of someone's old tree house. It's not. You were four. Mary came home early from work one day and she found him, having built a perch in the tree, and was sitting up there with his rifle. He was protecting the house because 'Charlie' was coming. That's what he told her and it scared the living daylights out of her. It was the last straw."

I covered my ears and kept walking, picking up pace. "I don't want to hear another word!"

"He was supposed to be watching you, Lucy, and you were playing in the front yard while he was up in that tree. She didn't let him watch you too often because she was always afraid that he might snap or run off as he did from time to time. The one thing he was responsible about was usually you. That day he did what she always feared he would, he let his demons come before you."

"Stop! Just stop!" I screamed. Even with my ears covered, I could still hear him.

Mr. Watson didn't stop. "That's when Mary told him she was leaving him and taking you. He threatened her. He told her that he was the one that always took care of you while she was working. In his mind that was the truth and he told her there was no way she was taking his baby away from him."

"She was leaving him to protect you. What did she have to fight him with but the truth? She told him he wasn't your father."

I spun on my heels and slapped him. I slapped Boyd Watson right across the meat of his cheek and my hand stung and twitched. He didn't even flinch. I covered my mouth with both hands. I felt nauseous. I knew there was something between them, but I never suspected.

Mr. Watson barely took a breath. "Two days later, the very day she enrolled you in daycare, he came by and checked you out. Took you to lunch at Michael's restaurant and then back to the house..."

"You killed him! The both of you killed him!" I screamed and he grabbed me in his arms as I sobbed. I jerked to get away, but he didn't let go. "You killed him!"

"I know, my sweet girl, and I'm so sorry. I never thought. I'm so sorry."

Tears streamed down my face.

Mr. Watson grabbed me and held me. "It's was never your fault, Lucy. It's always been mine and I'm so sorry. If I hadn't been desperate to save Lily or if I'd been a stronger man. I told you I've spent a lifetime trying to make it right, but all I seem to do is screw things up for you. I would have never sent you to the kennel if I had known what Dwayne Richards might do. You must believe me."

I sobbed uncontrollably.

"I was at the hospital the night you were born. I was the third person to hold you, even before your grandmother. You looked so much like Lily that I was afraid everyone would know, but at the same time I didn't care. You were mine and if the whole world knew, I wouldn't have cared. Mary was different. She didn't want our families to suffer the scandal or for you to have that sort of start in life."

Lila died a few weeks after you were born and you are what got me through the loss. Every single

183

time Lily got sick, thoughts of you, thoughts that you might need me, is what got me through it. I know you don't need me. I know you hate me and that makes me sick because I love you and Lily more than anything."

I just cried. "Don't say that! You don't love anyone, but yourself!"

"I'm so sorry, Lucy, but I don't regret you and I never will." He kept repeating, "I'll never regret you. I'm sorry I haven't been the father you deserve and I'm sorry we kept this from you."

"I want to go home," I lied. I didn't ever want to go home again, but I wanted to be away from him.

Chapter 12

I functioned in a haze. I got up in the morning. I went to the kennel. I worked and I came home. A couple of days went by like that.

I no longer looked to the hunt barn for glimpses of Edward. I no longer looked at my mother either. I no longer looked at anything the same. I couldn't shake the fact that all that I knew to be true about my life was now a lie. No wonder she never wanted to talk about my father, I mean, the man I thought was my father.

"What is wrong with you?" Edward chastised me. "Straighten your back, tuck your butt and lift from your heels! Jesus, Green, you know this!"

I dropped the reigns and jumped down off of Blueberry and walked off the field. I slung the riding crop blindly about as far as it would fly. I didn't say a word. I just kept walking. I left Edward standing there with the horse.

"Green!" He called after me, but I kept going until he caught up with me. "What is going on with you?"

I wiped my eyes. "Dwayne did something to your sister when she was here, didn't he? That's why you warned me about him. You said she went home early that summer, that's why, isn't it?"

"What does that have to do with anything?"

"Did he or didn't he?" That's where all this started. I should have just asked Edward to begin with instead of going to the Watson's that night.

Edward ran his hands through his hair. "Mainly he just said stuff to her. He scared her. He seemed to think they were an item, but he never acted on it."

"I should have just came to you and asked you the other night." I spun around and started toward the kennel.

"Green, wait."

"My name is Lucy!" The things that made me Green were all being chipped away. I should have seen the truth about myself, my parentage years ago. Only a fool wouldn't have known.

Again Edward came after me. He got out in front of me and wouldn't let me pass. "I'm not letting you go until you tell me what's going on with you."

I held my head in my hands and then shook them off down to my sides. "Just move!"

"What happened to you?"

"Move!"

"No!"

"I just wish I could be back under the Halfway House with you. That was the best night. We agreed we wouldn't pursue this because of my age and because of Lily. Did you know she's my sister? Am I the only one in the world that didn't know?"

"What? No."

Edward looked from side to side to see if there was anyone around watching us. "Come with me."

He took me by the hand and I let him. He was the first person since Monday night that I had allowed to touch me. I wasn't in a condition to feel anything, but then there was Edward. He was the beaters and my insides were cake batter around him.

Edward led me to the apartment above the hunt barn, even checked once more as we went up the stairs to make sure no one saw. He closed the door behind us and for a moment it was my birthday again.

The feel of his fingers in my hair made all of my cares start to slip away. The feel of his lips on mine, so soft, and the graze of his nose over my cheek as he pulled me closer was light as a feather and made me wonder how I'd ever thought I could stay away from him. Everything about us was a contradiction.

"Now you're going to tell me everything," he said as he eased away and led me to the couch.

Edward sat down first and patted the spot on the couch next to him. When I sat, he pulled my legs around and over his.

I told him every detail of my evening with Mr. Watson.

"When he took me home, Mama could tell just by the look on my face that he had told me. She was so mad with him that she made him walk home and he did. He left the Mustang. He could have taken it home and returned it later, but he left it and walked all the way from our house halfway across town at 10:00 p.m."

Edward didn't say much. He just listened.

"I can't help but think about what they did. They made a deal and that's how they had me. I was supposed to be a means to an end for both of them. I mean, did they just shake on it and get it on right there in his office or did they go to the Admiral?"

The Admiral is where all of the married men in Thomson took their mistresses. That was the worst kept secret in town.

"I guess that explains why so many people have said Lily and I look so much alike that we could be sisters. Makes sense. We are sisters."

My mind jumped from one point to another and from one question to the next. "Do you think we look alike?"

Edward was cautious, but answered, "Yeah, you kind-a do."

"I am such a fool. You are right to call me Green."

"I won't call you that anymore."

I took Edward's hands in mine. "No, I'm sorry. I didn't mean to yell at you while-ago. I like it when you call me that."

Edward just smiled and blinked with lashes that any woman would have killed for. My heart was breaking at that very moment just looking at him and knowing that I would have to put the distance back between us as soon as I left the apartment. As a defense mechanism, my mind switched back to the subject that brought me there. I was absolutely furious with my mother.

The thing I conveyed to Edward was that I was so frustrated. I was never allowed to be mad with my mother. In the last few weeks I'd seen a change in her. Until Mr. Watson's revelation, a new rapport was going on between Mama and me, but now I felt as if everything was undone.

If ever I wanted to be able to tell her I was furious with her it was now. I learned early on that there was no need pointing out any fault in her because it was promptly pointed out that my faults were always bigger and more bothersome than hers.

"'Who do you think you are?' was a common response to any grievance I aired and that was immediately followed with 'I'm the parent and you're the child.'" I explained to Edward and he covered his mouth.

"Of course you can't believe it," I continued. "She's usually on her best behavior in public, but behind closed doors, well I never let the conversations go any farther as it would always end badly for me."

I went on to tell him how I lived my life in silence, hiding out in a room where my father hung himself. He gasped over that one.

"I was caught square between her denial and bitterness and you're only the third person I've ever breathed a word of my true feelings to."

"The first person I told was my grandmother, Nanny, and I didn't tell her the full story. She tried talking to Mama, but that got me three spankings in one day for what Mama said was telling lies on her."

"When I was twelve, I worked up the courage to tell Maggie, my best friend that you met at my birthday party. I swore her to secrecy and she's never told a soul, but she started making every excuse to invite me to spend the night at her house. That was working out well until Mama finally realized that letting me go that often might make her look like a bad mother."

"Maggie and I thought we would solve the problem by having Maggie spend the night with me, but the ceiling fan that my father used to kill himself still being in my room gave her the heebeejeebees."

I snapped out of my walk down memory lane and redirected my fury to Mr. Watson. "I could just scream at him for ruining the change in Mama. I'm furious with him for not marrying her years ago and maybe taking the edge off of her..." "And you're furious with him for not saving you from her?" Edward asked.

I had never been mad like this before and certainly not for so long. I was exhausted from it and I could hear it in my voice when I let out the word, "Yeah."

There was a moment where neither of us said anything and then I felt the need to back-pedal a little about Mama. "You know, she's not all bad. I do have some fond memories of life with her. I feel like I shouldn't just tell you the bad stuff."

"She was great at swimming lessons. Most of the kids I knew, their dads took them to the end of the dock and pitched them in. It was sink or swim for them, but not me. She couldn't have been more patient and it took two summers for me to fully get the hang of it and she never once pressured me or complained."

"When I was sick, she was the best. Every time I got sick she acted as if I was the most precious thing in the world and she was mortified she was going to lose me. Maggie got one of those twenty-four hour stomach bugs one time and her mama lost her mind and threatened to leave home for good if Maggie didn't keep the Kaopectate down. Who can keep that stuff down? The taste alone when you're not puking your guts up is enough to make you gag."

"She was a good mom. She was never a great mom, but she could have been. I saw a glimpse of her greatness in these last two weeks, but now here we are."

Edward appeared lost in thought for a moment. He stroked the back of my hand and ran his index finger down each one of mine on my right hand. "Do you think the reason your mother is the way she is over this is because she has lost all ground with teaching you right from wrong and that she's lost all control?"

"What do you mean?"

"You know the worst thing she ever did and she couldn't control how that information was delivered. It's likely that she fears you will never take her word for anything ever again. How will she be able to teach you right from wrong if you know what she has done? I'm not saying that's the attitude that you would take toward her, but I think that could be a factor for her."

"You imply that she thought she was perfect before."

"Think about it this way. She's always told you not to do drugs, right?"

I didn't really know what doing drugs had to do with this, but I played along. "Right."

"What if you found out she smoked a lot of pot? Would you ever take her word on not doing drugs again?"

"No. I guess not."

"That's my point. You've found out that she's done a great wrong so in her mind she's failed you on every level. Do you think when she and Mr. Watson first concocted this plan she ever thought your dad would kill himself? This was something no one was ever supposed to know, but here we are."

"I understand what you're saying, but I don't know what to think."

Edward casually looked at his watch. "I've got to get you back to the kennel before Mrs. Pope starts to look for you."

"I wish I could just hide out here until all of this blows over."

"There's nothing to hide from." He ran a finger through the strand of my hair that had fallen in my face and tucked it behind my ear. "You're still you and your parents still love you. That hasn't changed. You said he told you he didn't regret you. That's saying something, Green."

I smiled at the return of my nickname. "I guess."

Edward was right. I needed to get back to the kennel or Mrs. Pope would come looking for me. Ever since the episode with Dwayne she didn't like to let me out of her sight. Plus, how would it look if someone caught me up there with Edward alone?

I stood from the couch. "I should get going."

"Green." I turned back to Edward to see what he wanted. "I'd like to kiss you one more time before you go."

I blushed.

When I returned to work, Mrs. Pope acted as if she hadn't missed me at all. She didn't say a word to me about it. My mother went another three days before she said anything to me about Mr. Watson. She didn't go back to work all week and acted as if she hadn't missed a beat.

Chapter 13

"Lucy!"

The sound of her voice startled me and I sat straight up in the bed. I don't know when I expected her to crawl out from under the covers, but Saturday morning at 7:00 a.m. wasn't it.

"Get up and get dressed!" she screamed.

I was so happy to hear her voice, sounding close to normal, that I didn't even bat an eye about being woken up that early. I was fully clothed and in the kitchen within about fifteen minutes.

"We're going on a road trip," Mama explained as she stuffed beach towels in a duffle bag. "Go get your bathing suit."

"Where are we going?"

"The beach."

"We're going to the beach?" The beach meant Tybee Island. The few times we had been to the beach, that's where we went. Mama liked to keep things in state.

"Yep. You, me and the Mustang. You wanna drive?"

"Okay."

We were on the road with in minutes and, short of the music from WSGA playing on the radio, the car was silent. She looked more like herself with the exception of puffy raccoon eyes, but she was still quiet.

"Are you alright?" I asked her.

"I've just had a week's vacation, shouldn't I be alright?"

"I meant you never stay home like that and I don't think you've ever done anything spontaneous in your life."

"That's not true. I've done something spontaneous before."

"Name it."

"Lucy Meeks."

I wasn't sure how much I wanted her to elaborate, but she seemed open to talking about it.

"Would you like to tell me your side of things?" Talking with Edward had calmed me down a bit about the whole thing. "You don't have to if you don't want to."

Thirty miles down the road, Mama finally found her words.

"Well you know now that I'm not perfect, but I'm still your mother," she began. "I'm sorry life didn't deal you a better hand and I'm sorry I haven't helped the situation."

There was a long pause, but I didn't dare say anything.

"I'm sure Boyd gave you an overview." She rolled her eyes. That was the first time in all my life that I could remember my mother rolling her eyes.

"I'm sure he mentioned that I was homecoming queen, but you knew that already, and I'm sure he told you we met the night I was crowned. I'd be willing to bet he didn't give you the details though."

"Of course I had a date that night, but he didn't care. He had his cousin introduce us and he also paid his cousin ten dollars to 'accidentally' spill punch on my date. When poor Bobby Harper went to get cleaned up, Boyd walked right up to me. I still can't believe what he said. I mean, the nerve."

"He said, 'When I was eight I wanted a bicycle and I got it. When I was sixteen, I wanted a Ford Mustang and I got it. I'm eighteen and I want you.'"

"He was so cocky and good looking it made me weak in the knees. He got me."

Telling me Boyd Watson was cocky was no shocker as that is how I'd always seen him.

"Did you love him?" I took a chance and asked her while she clearly reflected on the moment when she met Mr. Watson.

"More than you can imagine."

"And his mother came between you all."

"I'm sure that's what he told you, but the truth is, he came between us." Mama shook her head. "And I came between us. Neither one of us fought for us, but we were young and stupid. She said she'd cut him off and he thought that would make a difference, but I'd been poor all my life so it was no big deal for me. I never told him that and he never told me it was his mother, but I knew. I knew and it didn't matter because he wouldn't stand up to her."

"It was hard. You'll fall in love one day Lucy and you'll get your heart broken and you'll see. It happens to us all. We pick ourselves up, dust ourselves off and move on as best we can. I'm sorry I didn't do such a good job with moving on. I thought I did and then Boyd moved back to town. Compound that with your dad, I mean . . . Robert's problems. I gave in to temptation. I convinced myself that what we were doing, creating a baby, was a chance to help both of us, but I knew it was wrong."

Mama immediately tried to soften the blow. "I don't want you to think I didn't want you. I did, but the way I went about getting you was wrong. I've known that all along, but I never thought. Well, that's just the trouble, I didn't think at all. I didn't think about everyone else that was involved and how it would affect them and in that moment, all those years ago, I didn't think of you and I'm so sorry."

Mama reached over and took my hand from where it rested on the gear shift. "I am truly sorry, Lucy."

I didn't know what to say.

"I should have been the one to tell you and I'm sorry Boyd took that on himself. He's been wanting to tell you for years, but..."

"But you never wanted me to know." I tried to say that without blame or accusing her of anything.

"I know how it sounds, but no, I didn't want you to know. I know I haven't been the best mother, but

I tried and I didn't want you to know that I failed you even before you were born."

I took my chances and added my two cents. "I don't mean to criticize, but it's like you've been playing defense and Mr. Watson's been playing offense all my life. You two have raised me like the pig skin in a football game."

"What a way with words you have." Mama cut her eyes at me.

"We're going to do better, Lucy. I promise."

"Mama, did you call him at all this week?"

I had never felt sorry for Boyd Watson until this week. He called almost every hour on the hour. At first I took messages for her, but after the first couple of days, I let the machine get it. He was devastated. She had devastated him. All this time I thought it was Mama who couldn't live without him, but I think the way she had been all my life over him paled in comparison to how he was over her.

"No, I didn't talk to him all week." She pulled at a thread on her shorts and snapped it loose, definitely more interested in it than in Mr. Watson.

"Are you going to talk to him? Are you going to call him back? Are you going to go back to work? What are you going to do?" I rattled off one question after the other and didn't give her a chance to reply in between.

"I don't know."

"I know you love him."

Mama just looked at me. "What do you know about love?"

What did I know about love? Not a whole lot.

I knew I loved her despite herself. I loved her because she was my mother. I loved her for finally telling me the truth. I loved her for sparing me the gory details of her affair with Mr. Watson. I loved her for our trip to Tybee Island and for pointing out every cute boy that passed us. I loved her for being oblivious to the fact that I loved Edward.

As I looked at all the boys that passed by our towels on the beach, not a one of them remotely interested me. One had blue eyes, but Edwards were bluer. His were so blue they almost lacked color altogether.

One boy was a little taller, but he was thinner than Edward. Edward had muscles. When I leaned into him it was like leaning into a rock with one of those egg crate things over it, the thing Mama put over my mattress so she could get little more life out of it.

Another boy, well, Mama said he looked like Mr. Watson when he was young. Same hair color and haircut she pointed out. That was enough to make my stomach churn.

Yeah, I knew enough about love to know that in the middle of the chaos that was my summer, I had fallen in love with Edward. I never did answer Mama's question. I kept that to myself.

The real question was could I ever love Mr. Watson? Could I ever think of him as my father? I only had the memory of my dad, Robert Meeks, and I had loved that memory all my life. He was a war hero and, wherever I went, people remembered him fondly, not like Mama and Mr. Watson described him. He was kind of an icon for McDuffie County and that made me feel special.

Of course, everyone knew what happened to my dad. Most folks thought the war caught up with him. They call it post-traumatic stress syndrome now, but most folks around still refer to him as being shell shocked. They were partly right, but now I knew my true paternity was the best kept secret in town and a kept secret in these parts was pretty dang amazing.

There wasn't a cloud in the sky and there was a slight breeze coming off of the water. Mama wore a wide brimmed straw hat and had me lather her up numerous times to keep her fair skin from burning. I always knew I didn't take after Mama's side of the family with my skin that was so easy to tan. I assumed I took after the Meeks side, but now I knew better. I took after the Watsons. How strange it was to think about that. Everything I knew about myself was re-evaluated as I laid there on the beach.

"Mama, tell me the story of Daddy again," I flipped over on to my stomach.

Mama lifted the hat from over her face and looked at me. "Seriously? You want me to tell you that again?"

"Yes, please."

Mama gave a summary of Robert Meeks' time in Vietnam. "Robert Meeks was the second of three boys born to Ryland and Louella Meeks of Dearing. His brothers Ryland Jr. had a heart murmur from birth and escaped the draft due to his poor health. Robert was drafted and, his younger brother, Richard volunteered, but was told by the sergeant at the draft office that anyone crazy enough to volunteer to go to Vietnam wasn't fit to serve. He was dismissed and his draft forms discarded. The three boys were all full of pride, pride for their country and pride for their family name. The older and younger ruled useless to their country and essentially shaming the family name, Robert felt he had something to prove and something to make up for."

Mama rolled over and continued. "I didn't know him before he came home from the war and I've told you that before. I can't tell you what he was like before. I can only tell you what I've heard."

"Tell me about when you first met." She'd told me the story a million times before, but I wanted to hear it again.

"I had a job for a while waiting tables at Michael's. Your grandmamma was the one that trained me. Well, she tried to train me. I was terrible. I only got the job because the owner new my daddy and Daddy probably begged him."

"One day, I was spilling drinks and slinging plates, that's what I did more than fill glasses and serve lunches. Anyway, one day, in walks this young man, he wasn't in uniform, but every man in the restaurant saluted him, shook his hand and thanked him for his service. It was a sight and so was he. He wasn't bad on the eyes. He asked for Louella. One thing led to another and before I knew it we were married."

"That fast?"

"That fast. He seemed great at first. Good looking, charming and folks lined up to buy him drinks, lunches, dinner, you name it. As many times as you've made me tell you the story, I heard it every day and twice on Wednesdays and Sundays. While wounded, a clean shot through the hip and a graze across his scalp, three inches above his left ear that left a scar like the parting of his hair, Robert Meeks drug four other wounded soldiers from the jungle. It was a big battle, tons of casualties. It was just before the fall of Saigon. The war ended and he stayed on in the army for a little while. He seemed fine, but the gore he saw, no one can live through that unscathed."

Mama stopped and fell silent to her thoughts.

"Did you ever love him?"

"I think I did at first. He wasn't a bad man. He just got to where he couldn't help himself." Even to this day, Mama made excuses for him and I was always okay with that.

Mama and I laid there on our beach towels, each as lost in our thoughts as the other.

"So saving four soldiers was the most significant thing he did?"

Mama raised up from her towel and looked at me curiously.

"What's the most significant thing Mr. Watson's ever done?"

Mama lifted her big Jackie Onassis sunglasses with one hand and reached over and took mine with the other. "He gave me you."

A tilt of her head, the hint of her gleaming white teeth, she was beautiful and I could understand why he never got over her. I couldn't see them, but I knew she smiled and it showed through her eyes.

I think that was the nicest thing Mama ever said to me.

Both of us laid back on our beach towels and continued to bake in the sun. I thought for a few minutes about what she said about Mr. Watson. A strange feeling came over me, one that I wasn't used to feeling about him. It was a feeling of guilt combined with feeling sorry for him. The way Mama treated him all week made me feel sorry for him and the way I had felt about his constant interference all these years made me feel guilty. I understood now that he was doing his best to be as much of a father to me as Mama would allow.

"I guess he's not all bad," I said just loud enough for her to hear.

"No one's ever all good or all bad, Lucy. Most everyone's just doing the best they can in hopes that it's good enough. Boyd and I are no different." That's was the first time she ever admitted that there was a chink in her armor.

I thought about what she said and how I was so furious with her earlier in the week and how she was furious with him. I felt a little sorry for her too. As I laid there I pictured the young girl she once was and wondered what her life would have been like if Mrs. Watson wouldn't have interfered with her and Mr. Watson. Would young love have run its course or would they have stayed together? Would they have been like Maggie and the boys she dated, madly in love for six months or so and then on to the next or would they have been like Nanny and Papa, together from age sixteen until he died at sixty-three?

If they had stayed together, things would be so different. Would Lily and I exist? Would my dad be alive?

More questions came to mind. Would I always refer to Robert Meeks as my dad? It seemed disrespectful of his memory to stop. All of his family, his parents and both of his brothers were dead and I didn't know of any extended family. As far as I knew, I was the only one left to remember him. Maybe it didn't make a difference to anyone other than me, but it did make a difference to me.

Right now, only a handful of people knew the truth and as far as I was concerned it could stay that way. If the Thomson gossip mill got wind of this, Mama's worst fears would come true. She'd be labeled the town harlot and I wouldn't be seen as any better. No, I wouldn't change a thing. Robert Meeks would always be Daddy to me.

I finally gave up on all of the deep thinking. Mama was asleep so talking to her was out of the question. I got up and wandered out to the water. I wandered out to about knee deep, knee deep until the next wave hit me and nearly took me down. I was scrambling to keep my balance when something touched my leg. I jumped to get away, thinking it was a jelly fish or something, but it was a boy about my age body surfing. I wasn't able to completely get out of the way and he took my other leg out from under me and I crashed in the waves. My feet went over my head and I was tumbled in the water like a shell. I sucked up half the ocean before a hand pulled me by the arm and stood me up.

"Are you okay?" a voice of a young man asked.

I sputtered and snorted and made all sorts of unladylike noises as I tried to clear my nose to breath before squeaking out the words, "Yes, thank you."

Once I got the sand and salt out of my eyes, I could see that this young man was the closest thing to Edward I'd seen all day. I blushed at the sight of him and the instant wish to see Edward, not the next best thing that was standing in front of me.

"I'm Allen." Another wave hit me as he said his name and he reached out and helped steady me.

"Lucy."

"Do you have a boyfriend, Lucy?"

"Aren't you direct?" I should have said yes, but I really didn't know if Edward was my boyfriend. That was a good question. I wished he was my boyfriend.

"Allen," a girl called from the shore. "Come on. I'm ready to go."

"That's my sister," he shrugged.

"You should probably go. Thanks for saving me."

Allen started backing up. "If I leave, you aren't going to drown now are you?"

I dug my feet into the sand and secured my footing. "I'll be fine. Thanks."

"You didn't answer the question," he reminded me.

"Yeah, I kinda do have a boyfriend."

"Of course you do. All the pretty ones are taken. Lucky bastard." Then he turned and ran to the girl that was waiting for him.

It wasn't much longer before Mama realized that our best effort with the sunscreen had failed. She was a lobster and it was time for us to leave before she ended up with full blown sun poisoning.

Mama didn't trust me to drive that far in the dark so she insisted on driving us home.

"I haven't driven this car in almost twenty years." She ran her hand along the paint as she walked around to get in.

Chapter 14

I wasn't burnt, but the sun had zapped me pretty good. We were hardly over the bridge that connected Tybee Island from the mainland when I was gone. Thinking of Edward or dreaming of him, I wasn't sure there was a difference. I couldn't wait to get home and make any excuse at all to get away, to go find him. My head flopped against the head rest and the miles ticked by, but I wasn't in the car. I was a hundred miles away wrapped in his arms. I wanted to kiss him harder, longer, more than I had thus far. I wanted to wrap myself around him and forget all of my family drama for a while.

The next thing I knew Mama was waking me up while turning into our driveway. I slept the entire three hours home.

"Look alive your grandmother's here." Mama poked me.

Nanny didn't wait for Mama to cut the car off before she opened the driver's side door.

"We've been searching high and low for you all." Nanny was in a panic.

"What's going on?" Mama said as she turned the ignition and then handed me the keys.

"It's Lily Watson. She's in the hospital and it's not looking good. She's asking for Lucy."

"And Boyd?" Mama asked. All of her anger with him instantly fell away.

"Oh, Lord, Mary, he's beside himself," Nanny shook her head. "Last time she was sick, he still had his mother and, well, you know." Nanny's implication was that he had Mama then. Nanny knew the events of the last week and how furious Mama was with him.

Nanny was firmly planted in the doorway and I thought that's why Mama hadn't gotten out, but that wasn't necessarily it. I opened my door get out, but Mama stopped me. "Get back in Lucy. We're going to the hospital."

Mama turned her attention back to Nanny as I followed her and handed her the keys back. "Which hospital is she in?"

"University."

Mama didn't bother to ask which room and Nanny got out of the way as Mama cranked the Mustang. Off to Augusta at nearly 9:00 p.m. we went.

Mama took the interstate and we made record time to downtown Augusta. There was hardly any time for conversation beyond Mama asking if Lily had said anything to me about the cancer being back.

"No, I thought she was fine. I was supposed to start teaching her to drive this week." I did my best to think of anything, but I didn't have a clue that she might be sick again.

"Lily wanted to learn to drive?" Mama barely took her eyes off the road to give me a curious look.

"She wanted to be normal. What she fails to realize is there's no such thing as normal."

Mama sighed sensing the attitude I had toward the concept of normal. She took a long hard look at me and added, "Whenever you think you've got it rough just think about her life."

As soon as she shut off the car, Mama rushed to the entrance of University Hospital at a full sprint with me trying following behind, doing my best to catch her. I didn't need the lights of the parking lot to see her. She was so red she glowed in the dark, but the burn that usually made her claw at her skin and run through every home remedy was the farthest thing from her mind at that point. She still had on her bathing suit as underwear and so did I, but she didn't seem concerned about that either.

Mama paused just long enough at the information desk to find out which room Lily was in and then she was at a run to the elevators.

"But, Ma'am, visiting hours are over, especially for ICU," the elderly volunteer manning the desk yelled after us.

"Sorry," I called back to the lady as Mama pounded on the up button to call the elevator.

The elevator was there in a split second, but that wasn't soon enough for Mama's liking. She paced back and forth twice before giving the button a few more pokes.

"I've got a bad feeling." Mama rung her hands in frustration. "Come on," she ordered the elevator.

It finally came and it took, what Mama called, "its sweet time," getting to the fourth floor. When the doors finally opened, Mr. Watson spotted us straight away. He was disheveled and he appeared to have aged ten years. His eyes were puffy and bloodshot and he looked utterly exhausted, but he ran to Mama much the way she had ran through the parking lot and lobby of the hospital moments before.

Mama opened her arms to him as he approached and Mr. Watson fell limp around her. Mama was just about as thin as I was and her frame could hardly support him. He was not quite two of her, but definitely bigger. Of course I'd seen him upset over Lily and the cancer before, but I had been spared seeing him like this. Most of the time Mama left me with Nanny for days on end while she stayed with Mr. Watson when Lily was sick in the past, she might have done the same this time had she known how bad off Lily was.

"I can't do this. I can't let her go." Mr. Watson sobbed and Mama just held him.

Nurses passing in the hall stopped to check on him, but even though she was struggling to support his weight, Mama waived them away. She didn't waive me away when I stepped up to help her.

"Let's sit over here." I gestured to the couch in the waiting area.

Mama nodded and, working together, we managed to get him over to the couch. The three of us plopped down together, Mama on one side of him and me on the other. Mr. Watson clutched onto our hands and began to explain that he had been there almost all day by himself.

"Edward got here about 3:00 p.m. I told him I didn't want anything, but he wouldn't take no for an answer and he's gone to pick up dinner for us. I can't eat. I just..." He broke off in tears again.

Mama eased her hand from his and put it around his shoulders. She held him until he could compose himself enough for her to ask what exactly was going on with Lily.

"What happened? I didn't know she was sick again." Mama prodded carefully.

I was as curious as she was so I listened attentively to make out what Mr. Watson was saying between his bouts with the Kleenex Mama handed him from the box on the side table.

"That's the thing. Last month she had the all clear. No cancer." He blew his nose and it sounded like the horn of the tugboat we'd heard as we crossed over the bridge from Tybee earlier.

"Then what's wrong with her?" I was the one with the question then.

Mr. Watson glanced at Mama, his eyes seeking approval to tell me. There was a definite instinct to continue to protect me from the truth.

Mama gave a speaking look for him to continue and he did.

"We were pulling weeds in the front yard. It was hot and I told her she didn't have to help me, but she..."

I completed his sentence. "She wants to do things that normal people do."

"Yeah, that's her," he admitted. "But, she's not like normal people."

He hung his head and we all waited for him, thinking he was going to cry again, but he didn't.

Mr. Watson started again. "You're right, Lucy. There we were pulling weeds. I gave her a bucket to sit on and she was doing a fine job. She was also telling me that she wanted to learn to drive and she was telling me that she had applied to Augusta State and she planned on starting college. She started, 'I'm going to major in,' and then she stopped. I thought she was just winded, you know the way she gets." He looked at Mama.

"I know," she acknowledged.

"So I thought she was just catching her breath, but when she didn't finish her sentence, I looked back and saw her. The bucket was flipped over and she was sprawled out in the yard.

Mama and I both gasped. I screamed her name and I ran to her. She didn't even flinch. Mr. Wilson from two streets over was walking his dog and he sure flinched. He's the one that ran in the house and called 911. She wasn't breathing so I did CPR. Mr. Wilson ran back out, he's eighty and he ran, told me he was a medic in the war and shoved me out of the way and went to work on her until the ambulance arrived. Can you imagine they couldn't find Lee Street?"

Mama and I both shook our heads. Everyone in Thomson knew where Lee Street was.

"They took her to McDuffie County and then life-flighted her here." Mr. Watson sniffled. "She always wanted to ride in a helicopter."

I looked up and there was Edward coming down the hallway.

I whispered to Edward, "What's a hematoma?"

"A bruise."

Mr. Watson tried to stifle his tears, but they kept coming and he tried to answer our question. "What happened to her?"

"She had a heart attack. After all the ups and downs and back and forth with Leukemia and Lily up and has a heart attack. Can you imagine? A heart attack. That's all they've said so far is that she had a heart attack."

There was an unspoken devotion between my mother and Mr. Watson. It wasn't evidenced by the years of tension between Mama and me over him. It was evidenced in the way she laid her head on his shoulder and the gentle squeeze she gave his hand, a hand she hadn't let so of since she first emerged from the elevator. It was evidenced in the way she looked at him. His heart was breaking for his daughter and hers was breaking for him. It was in her eyes that if he hurt so did she.

It was only now that the truth was finally out that I finally saw them for what they were, long suffering at the hands of a mistake made years ago. Was the mistake me or was the mistake the easy way out that Mr. Watson took when he didn't defy his mother? Who knew? They'd both made mistakes and seeing them at the hospital like this, made me feel disappointed for them. The life they should have had was stolen from them and this is what they were left with, a life of struggles.

It wasn't a heart attack, but my heart definitely fluttered. It fluttered at the sight of Edward coming down the hall. Jeans, the same old white polo shirt, flip flops, he was the vision I had daydreamed about all day and he appeared at just the right time. Seeing him took the edge off of the gravity of the situation for me. The loss of Lily would devastate us all and I didn't want to think about that possibility. Edward was the light in an utterly dark evening.

Mama and Mr. Watson had their heads pressed together and hung so they didn't notice Edward acknowledge me. "Green," he mouthed and I mustered a sad smile.

Edward followed with a greeting to Mama. "Ms. Meeks."

Mama stood and hugged him. "Edward, thank you so much for coming down."

"Of course," he replied.

By the time Mama released Edward, Mr. Watson was standing by her side. Edward handed him the white bag. I couldn't see the logo, but I could smell what was inside.

"I know you said you didn't want anything, but you need to eat and it was the only place open."

The bag Edward handed Mr. Watson exuded the aroma of McDonald's French fries and a cheeseburger. I hadn't had dinner either and my stomach growled loud enough that everyone heard. My stomach said, "feed me," but my mind said, "don't you dare."

"Thanks, Edward, but I can't eat." Mr. Watson immediately passed the bag to me. "You take it, Lucy. I'm guessing y'all didn't have time to grab something before heading down here."

"No, thanks." I stepped back, refusing to take his food. I changed the subject. "Do you think I can see Lily? Nanny said she was asking for me."

"They were doing some tests on her earlier and that's how I ended up out here, but they might be done. I'll go check." As he walked away, Mr. Watson shoved the paper sack of fast food into me, forcing me to take it.

I sat the bag down on the coffee table. Mama followed Mr. Watson, leaving Edward and I alone.

"Have you seen her?" I asked Edward.

Edward reached for me and patted the back of my hand with comfort. "She doesn't look like herself. You should prepare yourself."

I threw myself into him and buried my face. I held on to him for dear life, for Lily's life. What if she died? Did she know we were real sisters like she'd always wanted us to be?

Mr. Watson came back and told me I could have five minutes with her, but visiting hours were over so after that I had to go home. Mama stayed with Edward in the waiting room and Mr. Watson escorted me back.

The waiting room was warm with brown and beige décor, a little burnt orange thrown in for good measure. There was carpet on the floor, the kind that one could sweep about as well as vacuum. Beyond the double doors was another world. It was cold and sterile. The walls were white and the floor was too. The only variation between the wall and the floor was that the floor had random flakes of baby blue. It was hard tile with a wet floor sign, mop and one of those rolling buckets propped against the wall between two doors to patients' rooms.

Mr. Watson led and I followed. We went a good ways down the hall, passing several rooms for patients. One of the room doors was open and my eyes wandered in as we passed. I only got a glimpse, but it was an elderly woman and she was hooked to a dozen tubes, big ones, small ones, all sizes. I wondered if that's what I would find when I walked into Lily's room. My stomach churned and I thanked the Lord I hadn't eaten anything since the ham sandwich from Mama's picnic basket on the beach.

The hall opened into a big room with the nurse's station in the middle. The walkway circled around the nurses and rooms with glass walls encompassed the outer space.

"You've gotta be real special to get one of the fishbowls."

As worried and concerned for Lily as he was, Mr. Watson tried to make light of the situation. I knew he only did that for my benefit.

Lily was in the second room around to the right. Even I knew "the fishbowl" as he called it wasn't a good sign. She didn't have the mass of tubes the lady down the hall had. She just had the tiny ones. There was a set of the standard nose tubes like you see every actor on TV who's portraying someone in the hospital has on. She also had an IV in one wrist and a few other thin ones coming out of the neck of her gown.

I couldn't take my eyes off of Lily. Even though my eyes were filling, I couldn't even stop looking at her to blink back the tears. She was ghost white and so still.

I tugged at Mr. Watson's sleeve to get his attention. "Can she hear us?"

"Lucy?" Lily stretched out her hand to me.

That answered my question. I went to her as fast as I could.

"Daddy, could you leave us?"

Mr. Watson gave a questioning look and Lily answered, "I'll be fine. Pull the door to on your way out."

218

Reluctantly Mr. Watson did as she asked and both Lily and I watched him all the way out the door. As soon as he was out of ear shot, Lily said her peace.

"He's going to need you now more than ever."

"What?" I gasped. "No! He needs you."

"I know you know and it's about time they told you."

"You knew?" Again, I gasped.

"You look just like a filled out version of me. Of course I knew."

"Do they know you know?"

"He does now."

"You know, we don't have to talk about this now."

Lily shook her head with exasperation. "There may not be another time."

I put on a brave face and wiped my tears away. "Don't be silly. You're gonna out live us all."

"Lucy, I'm being serious."

"So am I. I just found out that I have a sister and, if you think I'm letting you check out now, you're out of your gourd. So, suck it up, take a rest at this here swanky hotel and get your ticker back in order. You're not going anywhere but home and, as soon as you do, I'm teaching you to drive and we are going shopping. No sister of mine is going to be seen in the likes of this sad robe."

Lily couldn't help, but laugh. "You don't like my robe?"

"No, it's hideous. I'm going to write on your chart that they need to check your eyes while you're in here." I acted as if I was going to get the chart from its slot at the end of her bed.

"Lucy, all jokes aside. You need to make peace with Daddy and your mother. They deserve some happiness and you're the only one that can make that happen."

"I think you give me too much credit."

"They need you to be okay before..."

"You're the one that needs to get better, not me."

"I'm not talking about that. Just listen and let me be your big sister while I can." Lily reached for the tumbler on the bedside table, but she couldn't quite make it so I helped her. I waited with baited breath as she took two sips before starting again.

"You need to accept what you can't change." Lily took another sip.

"I don't understand."

"Fear that people around town would find out about who you really are is what's kept them apart all these years. The fear of what people would say and what it would do to you, that's...Well, it's in your power to let my daddy, our dad, be happy. Will you do that for me? You don't know him the way I do and he loves you and your mother more than just about anything and he's suffered enough."

"I don't know what I can do."

"You can tell them it's okay. You can accept what you can't change and you can no more change the past and their love and what they've done than all these doctors can give me one more day than the Lord wants me to have."

Lily made a good case and she was right. I think their suffering had only brought suffering to those of us around them.

The five minutes I had with Lily ticked by in a flash and before I knew it Mr. Watson stuck his head in the door. "Time's up. Come on, Lucy. You girls can chat some more tomorrow."

The look on Lily's face as I said, "See you tomorrow," was that of resolve. She had resolved herself to the suspicion that she was not coming out of the hospital alive this time. Her attitude and that look on her face is what made me turn around when Mr. Watson and I reached the double doors that separated the ICU from the waiting room.

"I'll be right back," I told him as he held the door for me.

In a restrained scream, one of the nurses chastised me. "No running!"

I paid no attention and rushed into Lily's room. "Hey!" I announced and her eyes popped open.

"I'll make you a deal. I'll accept what I can't change, as you put it, I'll even embrace him as my dad, but you have to get your head on straight and fight this."

Lily just looked at me wide eyed and I could swear I saw a bit of color coming back to her cheeks.

"You see," I added, "this thing I have to accept, you and me," I pointed back and forth between the two of us, "we're in it together. Deal?"

"Lucy, I'm not..."

"Deal?!!" I wasn't trying to be insensitive, but I figured she'd had enough of people pitying her. I decided to go with bribery and tough love.

"Deal," Lily said half-heartedly.

"Say it like you mean it and pinky-swear." I held out my pinky to her.

Lily crooked her little finger around mine. "Deal."

Chapter 15

"You're the only person I know that's probably ever talked to her that way," Edward chuckled at the end of the retelling of my conversation with Lily.

"I think she's spent her life with no one expecting anything of her and where has that gotten her? I think folks not having any expectations of her is the same as giving up on her and she's given up on herself. Maybe it will do her good to have someone expect something from her, even if it is just me."

"And what about your end of the bargain? Can you hold up your end?"

"Did I ever really have a choice?"

Edward tended to drive with his right hand resting on the stick shift. As we cruised along the streets of downtown Augusta, Edward's hand left the stick and reached over to where my hands were resting in my lap. He gave me a squeeze.

"I think you're doing the right thing."

Although this wasn't the alone time with Edward that I had imagined all day, but it was more than good enough. The touch of his hands magnified the chill bumps I already had from the breeze whipping through the Bronco. I was thankful, Mr. Watson insisted Edward give me a ride home and more thankful that Edward agreed.

Mama stayed behind with Mr. Watson and they had alone time too. Well, they had as much alone time as two people could have in the ICU waiting room. I had a feeling that it didn't matter if a thousand people were around, they would work things out tonight and they would go back to the way they always were.

Edward followed my directions and we took River Watch Parkway to I-20. In the middle of the clover leaf loop onto the interstate he cautioned, "Don't get your feelings hurt if sheer determination isn't enough to save her... She did have a heart attack, you know."

I almost ignored him, but instead I asked the obvious question that had been bugging me all night. "About that; did they doctors say what caused it? Heart attacks are usually for old people not twenty year olds."

"You're in luck. I happened to be standing there when the doctor explained it to Mr. Watson. Anyone can have the type of heart attack Lily had. Unlike the type that our grandparents and their friends typically have, Lily's wasn't caused by a lifetime of plaque and cholesterol build up. Hers was caused by a blood clot that traveled to her heart."

"What?"

"When you or I, a healthy person, gets a bruise, the dried blood that makes a bruise breaks down as it heals. It breaks down so small that the pieces pass through and are absorbed by the body. Sometimes, especially frail people, like Lily, aren't able to fully break down the bruise. In her case the giant bruise on the back of her right leg didn't dissolve and when the clot passed through her heart, it caused the heart attack."

On the ride home from the hospital and, despite Lily's condition and my frame of mind over it, the evening started to shape up as I had dreamed about all day. We talked about a hundred things like how he wanted to be a doctor and that he loved it here in Georgia so much that he planned to apply to the Medical College of Georgia for medical school. I told him that I wanted to go to UGA for as long as I could remember.

"It's strange now. I still want to go there, but it was more to fulfill a dream that my dad had than for me." I clarified to make sure he understood that I was talking about Robert Meeks as my dad and not Mr. Watson since Edward was one of the few people who knew the whole story. "He wanted to go to the University of Georgia, but the war came and that was the end of that."

"If you could study anything anywhere, what would it be?" Edward slid his hand from the gear shift to my thigh as he asked.

"I'd study drawing and painting in Italy."

"Then why don't you do that?"

"You've seen our house. It's not like we're busting at the seams with money."

"I have a feeling you have a great deal more at your disposal than you think."

"I guess you mean Mr. Watson's money? I don't want it."

Edward just smiled at me. "I think that's one of the things I like best about you. Despite everything, you know who you are and what's right and wrong. There's no real gray area with you, is there?"

"I'm glad someone likes that about me, but you're wrong. I'm about as lost about who I am as the next person."

We passed the Thomson city limits sign and a hush fell over the Bronco. Not another word was spoken and we were left with our thoughts until we pulled into my driveway.

We rolled to a stop just beyond the carport and Edward shut off the truck. "I'll walk you to the door."

Edward walked me to the door under the carport and waited as I let us in with the key Mama had given me. I wasn't supposed to allow anyone in the house when Mama wasn't home, but I invited him in.

The house was quiet and dark. I nervously searched on the wrong wall next to the door for the light switch before remembering it was on the opposite side. I flicked the switch and turned to the refrigerator. I fumbled over the words to offer Edward something to drink.

"A glass of milk would be nice," he replied as he retrieved the keys from the door where I had so absentmindedly left them in the lock.

I opened the refrigerator, took out the carton of milk and placed it on the counter. I stood on my toes and stretched to reach the good glasses in the cabinet. I didn't want to present Edward with one of the Smurf glasses that we had collected from Hardee's that Mama and I normally used. Just as I felt my fingertips make it to the goblets that Mama kept on the second shelf, I also felt Edward press against me and wrap an arm around me. He braced himself against the cabinet with the other.

It was a strange sensation being alone in the house with him like this. Ever since I got out of his truck there was a curious question as to what would happen next. Would he kiss me? If so, when? Now that question was being answered.

The hair on the back of my neck stood up as he planted kisses from my ear lobe down. Chill bumps covered my entire right side, down my arm and down my leg too. Edward's kisses were delightful as usual, but my mind wandered. I hadn't showered and I'd been on the beach for the better part of the day. Between the salt air and the sweat, I was sure he would be repulsed at the taste of my skin.

I pulled down the glass and sat it by the milk carton. I slipped in his grasp and turned to face him. My cheeks were flushed and I could hardly face him. There was a burning inside of me that felt like I wanted to eat him alive. I knew if I looked him in the eyes, I might not be able to squash that feeling so I looked at his chin when I asked, "Do you mind staying here while I take a shower?"

Edward looked defeated, "No, that's fine. I'll wait until you get out to before I go."

I hesitated, still not able to look at him, but out popped the words. "You could stay here."

"I don't know."

I didn't know either, but I'd never been home alone before and I certainly didn't want to be home alone now.

"If it's okay, I can make up the couch for you." I gestured to the couch.

"You get a shower and I'll think on it."

"Fine."

Once out of the shower, I tried on every set of pajamas I had before settling on a pink tank top and matching shorts. They were the most feminine set I had and probably the most revealing.

I dried my hair and it took the curl out which pleased me. I also resisted the urge to put on full make-up, but used my better judgement and just lotioned my legs and brushed my teeth.

I returned to the living room to find that Edward had made a pallet on the floor between the couch and the television. The coffee table was pushed off to one side and his decision to stay was clearly made as well.

Edward was twisting the rabbit ears on the television trying to get the stations to come in better, but not having much luck when I came in.

"It's funny, cloudy nights are the best. On a night like this, we can only get Channel 12." The nervousness was back and my voice shook a little as I gave the instruction.

The dial was on Channel 26 and Edward turned it to 12 and the station came in clear as a bell. When he finished with the TV is when he turned and got a look at me.

"Do you mind if I hang out here on the couch for a little while before I go to bed?" I asked.

"No, that's perfect." Edward slipped off his shoes and took a seat on the couch. "I'll sit with you."

Saturday Night Live was winding down. I snuggled into him as he wrapped an arm around me and we watched like that until it was over.

I didn't know what else to do so I said, "I guess I'll go to bed now. Thanks for staying with me," and I stood to leave, but Edward didn't let go of my hand.

"Lucy?"

"Yes?"

"Do you think we'd get caught if you slept out here?"

My knees went weak over his question and that feeling of wanting to eat him alive was back. Even weak kneed, I nearly leapt at the thought of sleeping next to him. "I'm sure we'll wake up well before Mama comes home and, if we don't, we'll wake up to the sound of the Mustang pulling into the driveway."

"Then you'll stay?"

I squatted down on my knees on the pallet and gave Edward's hand a little tug to join me.

Once on the floor Edward mentioned, "I don't usually sleep in a shirt. Would it bother you if...?"

I didn't let him finish his question. I reached for the hem of his shirt and between the two of us we worked it up and over his head. I'd never been so bold in all of my life and I'd never seen him without his shirt before. Even on our knees he towered over me.

I tried not to look, but Edward had only the slightest bit of hair on his chest and most of it was a line that led from his naval down into the top of his jeans. The shape of his shoulders, the muscles in his chest, I'd never even imagined how he looked without his shirt, but I knew I'd never be able to think of anything else again.

I wondered what it would be like to feel his skin on mine so I inched closer to him. "Do you mind?" I asked as I started from his wrists and ran my hands up his arms. Edward didn't protest so I kept going, over this shoulder and down his chest. My fingers and palms flowed over his peck muscles and I was reminded again of flesh over rock. He was soft and firm all at once.

"Do you mind if I do the same?"

My insides quivered and I nodded my head, letting him know that I wouldn't mind. Not really knowing what to do, I let my hands rest at the top of waistband to his jeans.

Like I had done, Edward started at my wrists and worked his way up. My chill bumps were back. I was frozen with anticipation as his hands traveled over my shoulders. Was he going to take the same route over me that I had taken over him?

Again, my insides quivered and I could hardly hold still at the anticipation of his touch. Good sense was saying back off and not to let him touch me like that, but my body was saying otherwise. I held my shoulders back as he went over them and essentially offered him my breasts.

The material of my tank top was thin and for a second I looked down and could see my own nipples standing erect. Edward slid his hands down as I had done to him and over me they went. He lingered for a second and I leaned my face into his neck.

I was ever conscious about being forward with him, but I whispered, "I've thought about you all day."

Edward took my face in his hands. Before taking my mouth in his, he whispered back. "I think of you every day. I tell myself to stop, but I can't seem to think of anything else."

Deeper, harder, more intense than ever, that's how Edward kissed me. If he held me any tighter he would have pulled me inside of him. I reciprocated, clutching him as close to me as I could get him. His hands and arms roamed me and mine did the same to him. From the hair on the back of his neck to the inside of the back pockets on his jeans, my hands explored him. There were times when his hands were up the back of my tank top and tickling my back as they lightly went over my skin and there were other times when the muscles of my butt cheeks clenched as he caught handfuls of them and pulled me to him.

Finally, Edward braced a hand around my neck and one around my waist and we went down. My knees went up and instinct kicked in when I wrapped my legs around him. Through his jeans, my shorts and panties, I could feel his erection. I'd never felt such before.

Edward could have taken my virginity and I'd have gladly given it to him, but he didn't. I burned for him and I ached for him. Just from his kisses I cried out his name, "Oh, Edward," in a breathless sigh especially when he moved down, cupped my breast in his hand and gently scraped his teeth through the material and over my left nipple.

"Too far?" he asked in response to my cry.

"No." My knees trembled, but I didn't want him to stop.

I didn't know how much he balanced above me, keeping his weight off of me with one arm while the other traveled down. He found the bottom of my shorts.

"I'll stop if you want me too," Edward offered.

I shook my head. Edward's eyes were bright and pleased. In that moment I lived to please him. I stretched up and locked my lips around his. As my tongue possessed his mouth I felt his fingers slip beneath the leg of my panties and, as he grazed my pubic hair a shiver ran over my entire body.

The graze turned into his full hand and again he asked, "Do you want me to stop?"

I leaned up and licked his Adam's apple, "Do you want me to stop?" I asked him the same question.

Edward gave a little laugh, "No."

"Good," I exhaled.

I licked is Adam's apple again as I felt his hand move lower into my panties and his thumb circled me. "My God, Lucy."

Edward bared his weight down on me a little and kissed my neck while his index finger slid inside. I gasped at the penetration, which was both shocking and exhilarating.

"Edward, haaaa," I cried out.

"I'm sorry, Lucy. I'll stop."

"Don't stop, Edward, don't stop," I begged him and opened my legs wider for encouragement.

"Are you sure?"

I reached down and undid the button of his jeans. "No, no," he cautioned me as he slid back into me and my breath caught again.

I was confused. "Don't you want to?"

"More than anything, but not tonight." Edward picked up a steady rhythm of sliding in and out of me and rubbing and I couldn't focus enough to ask why not.

The pit of my stomach knotted and release with the pressure and release of his touch. Something in me was building to a fever pitch. My heart raced and I was consumed and gave way to the most strange muscle spasms that left me breathless as I exhaled the Lord's name and his. "Good God, Edward." I wanted him to stop and not stop all at the same time.

The spasms, for lack of a better word, rolled to an end and I was spent beneath him. Edward continued to plant kisses along my neck while I wanted to wrap myself around him and never let go.

When I finally returned to my senses, I asked him, "Why didn't you want to?"

Again Edward reiterated his earlier answer that I had only half heard. "It's not that I don't want to, Lucy. It's that I shouldn't and I won't."

"I could touch you..." I eased my hand down to his jeans again.

"No, Lucy." Edward recoiled.

"But, why?"

I was starting to wonder if something was wrong with him. My mother always said that guys would do or say anything to get in my pants and I didn't think she meant getting in there the way I had just let him. I thought she meant all the way so when he refused, I wanted to know what was wrong with him or with me.

"Because I wouldn't be able to control myself." Edward rolled over on his back and pulled me to him.

I laid my head on his chest and listened to his heart beat. It was still slowing from a race the same as mine was.

"Lucy, you're just sixteen and your father would kill me. We're not even supposed to be together. What if Lily found out?"

Just when my heart was breaking, thinking he was having second thoughts, he went on. "I don't like sneaking around. I want everyone to know you're my girl, but that's a luxury we don't have right now."

Chapter 16

There are things that I could remain blissfully ignorant about all my life and how Lily came to have the bruise on her leg that led to the blood clot that caused her heart attack; that was one of those things. In what started as casual conversation, Edward told me how it happened. Our talk ended in quite a heap of emotions on my part. I'm sure now that he wished he hadn't, and if he had it to do over again, he wouldn't.

The dream of being Edward's girl had been mine since the night I first laid eyes on him after the movies. He might not have known it, but I had been his girl all along. For him to say it, for him to want everyone to know, that thrilled me to pieces.

Of course I knew he was right. No one could know. The same old reasons kept us sneaking around plus the situation with Lily was worse. Her heart was medically broken. I'm not sure she could stand it being emotionally broken as well. Lily adored Edward as much as I did and, although I wanted him, I knew as well as he did that neither of us wanted to hurt her.

I was drifting off to sleep with thoughts of Lily weighing on my mind. On the ride home Edward and I rehashed what the doctors said happened to cause Lily to have a heart attack, a bruise that didn't dissolve and produced a clot.

I aired my thoughts out loud. "I wonder how she got the bruise in the first place."

It was well after 1:00 a.m. and apparently Edward was as awake as I was and he answered. "She fell down the steps at the hunt barn."

"What? How?" I twisted to see his face.

Edward brushed away the few strands of hair that had flopped in my face. "Lily was supposed to ride in one of the trucks when we took the hounds out on Wednesday afternoon. Molly dropped her off about thirty minutes too early. She thought she would hang out with me until everyone else showed up. When she didn't find me in the stables, she climbed the stairs to the apartment. She didn't find me there either because I had met up with the other whips for lunch at Neal's Bar-B-Que. I actually turned into the gate at the club just in time to see her fall."

"You saw her fall?"

"Yeah. It was pretty bad. I gave it the gas and tried to get to her as fast as I could."

I don't think it registered with Edward how deeply I despised Whitney Knox or he might have left the story at him going to help Lily. Instead he kept going.

"I think every member of the hunt knows where the spare key to my apartment is and a number of them let themselves in and use the place for various *reasons*." Edward emphasized the word "reasons" and gave me a wink. I knew what he meant.

"Half of them don't even bother to change the sheets and that's why I've taken to sleeping on the couch."

"That's awful!"

"Well, Whitney is a regular up there."

"I can imagine."

I went on to tell Edward about finding her in the horse trailer. His comment on that was, "Figures."

"Anyway," Edward got back on point, "Lily didn't find me in the apartment. She found Whitney and Whitney led her to believe that the other soul in the apartment, the one in the shower, was me. Lily was mortified, turned on her heel and made as good a run for it as she could. That's when Lily lost her footing and fell halfway down the stairs. Green, I'm telling you, I winced up just watching her."

I sat up. "I'm sorry, go back. You mean, Whitney caused all of this? She caused the fall that caused the, what was it called, hematoma, that caused the heart attack?"

I was fit to be tied even before he replied. "Not only did she start the chain reaction you just described, she didn't even bother to help Lily. Whitney stepped over Lily on the way down."

"Excuse me?!" I rung my hands and gritted my teeth. "Did you say she stepped over Lily?"

It was in that moment that I fully embraced the fact that Lily was my sister. If I had my own car right then, who's to say I wouldn't have driven over to her house and snatched Whitney out of her parent's house and beat her ass right then in the middle of the night? Whitney could mess with me all she wanted, she had almost all my life, but she was not messing with my family.

I hissed through my teeth, "I hate Whitney Knox!"

"Calm down, Green. Lily's going to be fine and everyone knows how Whitney is. Luckily, I came in when I did and was able to make sure Lily was alright and she knew I wasn't up there with Whitney doing..."

"Stop. I got it. I don't want that mental image." I rolled my eyes.

Edward was sweet, stroking my hand and coaxing me down, but I was determined that Whitney was not going to get away with this.

"I couldn't very well let Lily tell you that I'd taken up with Whitney Knox, could I?" Edward chuckled. "Come on now. Lay back down and let's get some sleep. I've never slept next to a girl before and I want to enjoy it."

I bit my lip and turned my face away to keep him from seeing me blush. His words rang in my ears, "I've never slept next to a girl before." I squealed inside.

Still hiding my excitement, I snuggled into his arm and pulled the quilt Nanny had given me over us. It probably went without saying, but I said it anyway. "I've never slept next to a boy before either and I've never been touched like that before."

239

I wanted to tell him that I loved him, but I held my tongue. I fell asleep that night plotting what to do to get even with Whitney Knox and knowing there was no getting even with her for nearly killing Lily.

The next morning I awoke with the dawn. I watched Edward sleep and marveled at how peaceful he was. He had recently had his hair cut. The sides were trimmed short, but he's left the top long. He wore it parted to the side and combed back, but this morning it was feathered across his forehead. I recalled that he'd never slept next to a girl before and reveled in the fact that I alone was fortunate enough to have seen him like this. He was beautiful and just looking at him made butterflies flutter in my stomach.

I didn't know how much time we had before my grandmother would come by to check on me. I prayed she'd call first, but I wasn't certain of that. What I did know was that it was 7:20 a.m. Sunday morning and daylight, but Nanny never went anywhere before 8:00 a.m. That meant I had forty more minutes with Edward and I wanted to make them count. After all, there's no telling when I might get another moment alone with him.

I ran and brushed my hair and my teeth. Then, I slipped back in our little make-shift bed on the living room floor. I snuggled into the space between his chest and his shoulder and I wormed my way up to his ear. I gave his earlobe a little nibble before I whispered to him, "Edward, do that thing to me again."

"Now that's a way to wake a fella up." Edward yawned, stretched and happily fulfilled my request.

From the moment Edward left that morning all I could think about was when I would see him again and when I would get my shot at Whitney Knox. I saw Edward at my riding lesson on Tuesday morning and afterward we had a moment together in Blueberry's stall.

"You smell like oats," I giggled as Edward pinned me against the back of the stall.

"Shhh...You smell like leather from the saddle, but I don't care."

Edward's kisses tickled and we had to cut it short when Mrs. Pope came looking for me.

"Lucy, I need to run to town. Come on and go with me," she called from a distance of a few stalls down.

On Wednesday, I got my shot at Whitney. I knew she'd be going out with the hunt that afternoon so I decided I was going out with the hunt as well. Lily had just been let out of the hospital that morning and I went by to check on her at lunch. I also used that opportunity to tell Mr. Watson that I was going out with Mrs. Harper.

"Are you up for riding in the middle of the field?"

Mr. Watson was concerned about my riding skills as the back of the field, with the children and the beginners, is where I had been riding. Whitney rode with the middle of the field so that's where I had to ride.

The field is what they called the group of riders that followed the actual hunt. The master and the whips were the ones doing the actual hunting with the hounds.

"Oh, yeah, Edward and Mrs. Harper said I would be fine. She'll look after me."

They turned the hounds out at 2:00 p.m. and they caught the scent of a fox straight away. There was chatter on the CBs and the whips were fast behind them. My skills as a rider had definitely improved since my first lesson, but I struggled to keep up. My main struggle wasn't with riding, but with ducking and dodging the branches as the middle of the field went through the woods and kept a look out for the fox whereas the back of the field typically stayed on a logging road or in the middle of a pasture or something.

Mrs. Harper was holding the CB for our group. "Listen," she commanded and we all called our horses to a screeching stop.

The voice came over the CB and another voice followed. We were privy to a conversation between Edward, the master and Mr. Horton, one of the other whips. The last words we heard were Edwards, "He's headed toward the Quaker cemetery!"

We could hear the hounds barking behind Edward through the speaker and we could hear them getting louder. We had just passed the Quaker cemetery.

"Keep your eyes peeled!" Mrs. Harper told the lot of us. She pulled her horse's reigns and gave him a heel sending him running back in the direction of the cemetery.

Whitney was near the back of the herd and I had been right next to Mrs. Harper. I let everyone between us go charging by and was able to jump down before Whitney got her horse moving. I grabbed the strap along the side of her horse's face and held tight.

"What are you doing?" She demanded to know.

"I think your horse threw his shoe," I lied.

I made Whitney think I was checking one of his front shoes when I leaned under his belly, but instead, I undid the buckle that held the strap to keep her saddle on.

"Nope. Everything's fine my mistake. All is well. Sorry." I gave her horse a slap on the behind and Whitney a friendly waive.

Whitney twisted in her saddle as her horse picked up a cantering pace and yelled at me, "Stupid bitch!"

When she twisted the saddle dislodged and did exactly what I hoped it would do. It tossed her sorry ass right off of her horse.

"Who's the stupid bitch now?" I screamed back at her as she rolled head over heels into the woods. It skipped her like a rock. I thought it was awesome.

Whitney's horse went galloping off and that thrilled me even more. Now she was going to have to walk back, that's what I first thought anyway.

I sauntered over to where Whitney landed all ready to give her the what for about messing with my sister and dare her to say one word, but instead the hounds came rushing through with the master of the hunt, Edward and two other red coats with them.

"Whoa!" they called their horses just about in unison.

"Lucy, are you alright?" Edward was the first to ask.

"Whitney fell off of her horse," I explained about the same time as we all heard Whitney screaming, the kind of screaming one does when they are in severe pain.

Three of the men jumped off of their horse and ran to find her. Edward grabbed their horses and lingered back with me.

Edward cut his eyes at me and I gave him a smile and a wink. I didn't think she was severely hurt so I was pretty proud of myself. My smile was met with a concerned look as Whitney's screams became more blood curdling.

"Jesus Christ, Lucy, what have you done?" Edward covered his mouth with a hand and shook his head.

Whitney's left arm was broken in two places and the shoulder was dislocated. She left the woods that day in an ambulance and there was no time and no way for me to taunt her with my lesson about messing with my sister and getting what she deserved. Sadly, I was the one that learned a lesson that day.

Mrs. Pope, Edward and I spend half the night gathering up the hounds while the rest of the members of the hunt went to the hospital to see about Whitney. Edward and I spent the evening without a word said between us. Apparently he was a fan of the silent treatment.

"I'm not sorry, you know," I grimaced as we pushed the last hound into the stall.

Mrs. Pope was gone so there was no one left to hear my confession, but Edward and he didn't say a thing.

"Aren't you going to say something to me?" I snapped.

More silence as I followed him to the door and waited while he locked up. I tried to touch Edward, but he flexed and jerked from under my hand.

"Edward, seriously?"

Edward started walking toward the hunt barn and I continued to follow. Halfway across the parking lot that separated it from the kennel Edward stopped and not so much turned around, but turned on me.

"Do you know what you've done?" Edward barked, towering over me.

I slinked back. His eyes were a blaze and he scared me. I was afraid not to answer, but couldn't form words. I shook my head.

"I saddled her horse today! She's blamed me! You're home free and I'm on the verge of being fired over your stupid prank!"

"I'm sorry, Edward." I started to cry.

"You're not sorry! You said so not two minutes ago. And, dry the damn tears up!"

"I am sorry!" I whimpered.

"I'll tell you what you are and it's not green anymore, that's for damn sure. You knew exactly what you were doing and you didn't think of anyone but yourself."

Edward stormed on to the apartment over the hunt barn and I sat down on the bumper of the Mustang and cried until I had no more tears to cry. When I was all cried out I got in the car and drove to Mr. Watson's house. For once in my life I needed him to be my father and to do what fathers do, fix their daughter's mistakes.

I rang the bell and waited. When Mr. Watson opened the door, I could tell his heart sank over the sight of me.

"Lucy, what's wrong? Come inside." He held the door open for me.

I shook my head. "I don't want to disturb Lily."

"But, I can't help you if you won't come in and tell me what's wrong."

"Could we sit on the porch?"

"Sure." Mr. Watson nodded and pulled the door to behind him.

I walked back to the steps and took a seat on the front step and looked up, silently asking him to join me and he did.

The sun had set and all the neighbors were inside. Lee Street was quiet as I told Mr. Watson what I had done.

"Did you hear about Whitney Knox getting hurt at the hunt today?" I bit my lip and waited for his answer.

"Yeah."

"I did it. I heard she's blaming Edward for not saddling her horse properly, but he didn't have anything to do with it."

"Yes, I heard that she said something about him." Mr. Watson's face was covered with his emotions. He squinted his eyes and focused real hard to look at me when he asked, "What did you do?"

"I loosened the buckle that holds the saddle in place."

"Why?"

"Because she's been hateful to me all my life and because she caused Lily to fall and get the bruise that made her have a heart attack." I shrugged my shoulders and gave him more details about the fall and the mean things that Whitney had done to me as a child. I stopped short of telling him about the horse trailer incident.

"Oh." His face turned red and the veins in his head protruded a little the way they did when he got mad. "And you were defending Lily?"

"Not so much defending as getting even."

Mr. Watson raised his hands to his face and took a good long wipe with them. I think he was searching for something to say and trying to calm down when he just came out with it. "Well, I think you may have succeeded admirably at that."

I didn't know whether he was proud of me or disappointed. "Can you help me?"

"Help you what? Sounds like you've gotten away with it."

"I haven't gotten away with anything if she gets Edward fired and he..." I stopped myself before I told Mr. Watson that I loved Edward and was utterly heartbroken right now.

As it turned out, Mr. Watson was smarter than Mama gave him credit for. He might have been oblivious to Lily's chasing him before my birthday, but somewhere along the way he started paying attention and not just to Lily.

"You and Edward are," he hesitated before finishing the question, "an item?"

I didn't answer him. I stared at him blankly as if I was confused by the question. I didn't want to tell him the truth, but I didn't want to lie either.

"I'm guessing you are and that you've been sneaking around to keep from hurting Lily. That's almost admirable considering what you've done to someone else who's hurt her."

"Are you mad at me?" I was scared of his answer and that's the first time I really cared what Boyd Watson thought of me.

He took a moment to answer. "No. I've seen the way he looks at you when he thinks no one else is looking. He's a good boy. Too old for you, but a good boy. No, I'm not mad at you, but I can't say that I'm real happy about the situation either."

I leaned over on Mr. Watson's shoulder and started to cry again. "I don't think he's going to look at me like that anymore."

"I don't know what I can do to change that, but I can tell you that I won't let him get fired over this.

I don't know what Mr. Watson did, but he fixed it. Edward didn't get fired and not another word was mentioned to me on the subject of Whitney Knox. There was one thing Mr. Watson couldn't fix. He couldn't put me and Edward back together again. As far as I could tell we were about as broken as Humpty Dumpty.

The bonus of all of this was that Whitney Knox made herself scarce around the hunt club the rest of the summer. She had to find a new pool of old men to get her kicks. The downside was that Edward made himself scarce around the Watson house and he found somewhere else to occupy his time.

Mr. Watson told Mama about me and Edward and the joke was now on her.

"Who's the fool now?" He turned her words around on her and she was none too keen on that, but she did come around.

My mother was sympathetic to my broken heart. "It's not like I didn't have one myself when I was just a bit older than you."

The rest of the summer Mama tried her best to occupy my mind with thoughts other than Edward. She made me a bride's made in her wedding. That's right. Her broken heart was finally mended and her twenty-five plus year courtship was finally over. Mr. Watson put a ring on her finger and dared anyone to say a word about it. And, although none of us breathed a word of the secret, folks around Thomson finally started to catch on. Lily and I looked alike for a reason, but no one seemed to mind. It wasn't the scandal Mama had been so terrified of after all.

It was the final weekend of the summer before school was to begin again. At dusk, out by the point at Amity Park where Mr. Watson would sit in the swing by the lake and think and pray for Lily, my parents finally got married. There was a tent and a hundred people from town. Edward came and he brought my mother a gift and he danced with Lily. He had avoided me and I figured he would do the same here so I pretended not to notice him and tried not to feel that same old pull toward him. I pretended to hang on every word that Maggie who came as my "plus one" had to say. I was doing a real good job of pretending until Edward approached me and asked me to dance.

It was the last dance of the night. A thousand stars twinkled overhead and the blood moon shown brighter and bigger than I'd ever seen before. The band that was set up at the corner of the pop and lock dance floor played Frank Sinatra's "The Way You Look Tonight."

Mr. Watson loved Frank Sinatra and I'd heard a lot of it during my comings and goings at his house over the summer. I'd heard this song a hundred times, but no other time was like this. This time I didn't so much hear it as I felt it. I was back in Edward's arms and he sang along.

The song was winding down and he pulled me closer than I'd seen him dance with anyone else all night. "I'm sorry." I could feel the air tickle past my shoulder as his words floated past.

"Me, too." Using the hand that was propped on his shoulder, I wiped a tear from my eye.

The last few notes of the song tapered off and Edward backed away. "I want you to read this after I'm gone." He held out a folded sheet of paper to me. "Put it in your purse and read it tomorrow."

I took the note and Edward turned to walk away. "Wait," I called out to him. He stopped and gave me his attention. I blurted out, "I have something for you in my car."

"Okay," Edward was skeptical. He probably knew I was lying. I didn't mean to lie, but it was the first thing that popped in my head.

I gave Maggie a speaking look and she understood. Edward followed me and I led him down the trail toward the parking lot. We were a couple of feet from my car when I came clean.

"I'm sorry. I don't have anything in my car. I was just hoping," I bit my lip and paused working up the courage to finish the sentence.

Edward hung on my words.

"I was just hoping that maybe you would let me kiss you one more time."

I didn't have to wait for him to agree to my request. Edward stepped forward and took my chin in his fingers. So gently, just like before, he lifted my lips to his. I could feel myself under the Halfway house with him again. Before I knew it, it was over.

"Read the letter," Edward reminded me.

Parked only a few spaces over, Edward headed toward the Bronco, leaving me for the summer, possibly forever. He was just about there when I called out to him. "Hey, Edward."

He looked back at me once more.

I couldn't let him go back to Virginia without knowing. "I miss being Green."

"Read the letter, Lucy."

*The End... For Now*

Dear Readers,

Thank you again for giving your time to my books. I hope you have enjoyed this one and will, as they say, stay tuned for what lies ahead for Lucy and the rest of the Watsons.

I love to hear from readers and welcome you to reach out to me. Please feel free to let me know how you liked <u>When I Was Green</u> or any of my other books. You may reach me via reviews at Amazon.com, comments on my Facebook page for Author TS Dawson or via email through the Contact link on my website, www.tsdawson.com.

Thank you and I look forward to hearing from you.

Oh, and, while you wait for the next book in this series, please check out my other books:

Port Honor

In Search of Honor

And

The Price of Honor

*-T. S. Dawson*

www.ingramcontent.com/pod-product-compliance
Lightning Source LLC
Chambersburg PA
CBHW071142170626
46809CB00002B/728